Leo Madigan is a Merchant Seaman. He first went to sea at 16. By 21 he had tried being an actor, a Horse Guardsman, a husband, a monk, a psychiatric worker. He returned to sea and has been shipping out steadily for ten years. He was encouraged to write by winning a literary competition organised by the Seafarers' Education Service, and since then his stories, articles and poems have frequently appeared in the Service's magazine *The Seafarer*. He has also contributed articles to *Blackwood*'s magazine. *Jackarandy* is his first novel.

JACKARANDY

LEO MADIGAN

QUARTET BOOKS   LONDON

Published by Quartet Books Limited 1973
27 Goodge Street, London W1P 1FD
Reprinted 1975

First published in Great Britain by Paul Elek Books Ltd 1972

Copyright © 1972 by Leo Madigan

ISBN 0 704 31025 2

Printed in Great Britain by
Hunt Barnard Printing Ltd, Aylesbury, Bucks

For Eileen
and
W.M.

Sat. 27th

I don't know; depression and a sort of emptiness . . . a train in a
siding . . . a ship becalmed . . .

Boy, what a homecoming! What a welcome! The Immigration
geezer was in two minds about letting me in and the Customs
fella charged two quid duty on a thirty-bob watch.

And a month ago the papers wouldn't stop calling me a hero . . .

People still remember in Singapore anyhow. Last night with
those matelots at Changi waiting for the flight and that Air Force
officer's wife throwing herself at me like I was a movie star or
someone, really, leaving her husband and those braided pigs,
walking across the lawn to our table and chatting me up, purring
and running her fingers through my hair. Vanity put the Chuck-it!-
this-happens-to-me-every-day pose into gear but secretly of course
I was preening myself and spreading my feathers in front of the
lads.

It was rounded off nicely too because after a while she wandered
over to a clump of trees and stood there with her back to us,
vomiting I guess, but taking advantage of the sudden silence I got
the laugh when I said 'I'm a bit cagey about birds who stand up for
a piss'.

Fairly petty; hardly a boast. She was half drunk after all and then
for the next eighteen hours in that plane the Hero was a furnace of

nerves. Hell how I hate flying. If only there was something to do, something to engage the mind but those long stretches of inactivity crucify me. And that plane last night was RAF – no booze, no movies, nothing.

The first hop from Singapore to Guam wasn't too bad. I was pretty boozed up and plagued mostly by a fear of being afraid. But then eight and a half hours from Guam to Cyprus – eight and a half hours non-stop flying into an interminable dawn like some science fiction horror. And then we circled five times over Akrotiri before landing; circled and swooped and soared again and my fists were clenched and bloodless with the strain of trying not to shake and my face felt white too and cold and damp with sweat.

It wasn't that I was afraid of the plane crashing; at times I wished it would – anything to relieve that tension. Even the night the *Tidepond* exploded and went down in a wind strong enough to rip the world apart I revelled in the danger. I was frightened – who wasn't? – but it was a wholesome enjoyable fear, a challenge, and it brought out the best in a man. Not so that flying.

Didn't give a damn about the crisp cold at Brize Norton though I only wore jeans and flip-flops and a light Singapore shirt. I was first off that plane onto good British earth and swore I'd never fly again though an hour later in the pub by Swindon station the hero was agreeing with the matelots that it hadn't been a bad flight and that a man would put up with a lot more to be back to a pint of real bitter, and would they be putting some away in the next few weeks? And would the birds know they were home? Would they ever, and tra la la and Jack's a man to reckon with . . .

I'll tell you what, I'm bloody tired; not just tired but exhausted, drained, enervated. Yet I can't sleep. The bar's still open downstairs but I couldn't go another drink. Think I've a cold coming on too; probably caught it stepping out of that plane this afternoon. Felt pretty sick coming down in the train to Paddington. Felt even sicker when the taxi to this Seamen's Hostel cost £2.10. Looks like the price of everything's gone up since I've been away, what with this new pence jazz.

The problem is what to do now. Shan't be allowed to ship out till the bone sets properly which will be six more weeks the doctor in Singapore said. Suppose I could wangle a small job somewhere but I don't really need to work. There's a couple of hundred in the bank and there'll be odd lumps coming in from here and there. Reckon I stand to make more out of the old *Tidepond* rusting at the bottom of the South China Sea than if she was still afloat and I was to get another year's work out of her. Guess I'll stay here and try to interest myself in something. Trouble is as soon as one of the old crowd arrives I'll go straight on the booze and that'll be it . . .

What I need is a bit of discipline. Must have the weakest will in the world – especially when I'm on the booze.

2200 hrs. Insomnia. Fears.

Perhaps I have something like delayed shock.

Keep thinking of Eddie Coulson and that little laugh he gave when we reached the mine-sweeper, so full of relief and gratitude after those violent hours.

And the sudden truth as they heaved us up on the ladder . . .

It bugs me; it's like I'm on fire inside.

Have rung his missus half a dozen times but she doesn't answer. Wish she would; I'd kind of like to talk about it. Wonder if she got my card.

If it must obsess me I suppose I could try to write it all down; do an account of the whole night and try to sell it to a newspaper or something.

Sun. 28th

In bed, sitting up, writing in this Chinese exercise book, my knees serving as a desk. Central heating apparatus runs the length of the wall but it's cold as a marble slab. The East End day dull and sky-less so I've drawn the curtains and switched on all the lights. Scant cheer.

Dragged myself down to the restaurant at 0900. Ate nothing but put away five cups of tea. As she poured my fifth the testy shrew at the service hatch said 'Well I got no simpuvvy for you. Yous boys'll drink yuselves inta 'vgrave one uv vese days – wait 'n see.' Thought she was on about the tea. Then caught a glimpse of myself in the mirror and realised she meant the booze. And last night was the first time in years I never had a drink.

No decent papers at the reception desk so rather than settle for a News of the Screws I followed directions from the tannoy and went to Mass in the chapel.

Only two others in the congregation, an old fella and a cleaning woman, and they didn't look like Catholics either. Can't remember when I went to Mass last. We carried a naval chaplain on the *Tidepond* from Singapore to Hong Kong a few months back and I remember helping to rig an altar on the flight deck but was told to relieve one of the watchkeepers when the time for Mass came because he was a Catholic and I wasn't. An evil little bastard too. He'd have been seen dead there in his own time.

Several fellas sitting around the lounge after Mass but none I knew so rang Eddie's missus again Still no answer. Felt depressed and miserable. Returned to room and finished *Words*. It has made a big impact on me all the way through but this morning the mood was dead and I sweated heavily in spite of the cold room.

To the lounge again at lunch time. The bar was open and there were quite a few in though it wasn't very lively. I begin to despair of seeing anyone I recognise when suddenly there is SL grinning recognition with half a head of teeth He looks the proper hill-billy what with yellow braces hitching jeans over a red shirt and leaning back with his elbows on the bar – almost exactly as I last saw him at the pay-off desk of a banana boat two years ago.

'What you havin' Keiron?' he asks. Even his voice has a smile about it.

'Lager and lime. I'm suffering. What you doing with yourself?'

'Fly out job. Joe Shell.' He indicates the brown paper bag at his feet 'Waiting on a cab.'

'The Gulf?'

'Singapore as far as I know. Cheers.'

We chat a while then the tannoy announces his taxi He picks up the brown paper bag and, still grinning, pokes a finger at my chest. 'See you, cock . . . an' leave me a virgin to come back to willya . . .'

I watch him stride through the lounge and out through the glass doors into the waiting cab to be whisked off to his aeroplane and Singapore and I imagine him arriving back in six months' to a

4

year's time with the same brown paper bag and braces and grin and I feel thoroughly abject.

Couldn't drink the lager – it refused to go down.

Rang Eddie's missus again – she must have moved or something.

Came back up here and turned in hoping to sweat out the worst of the fever and sleep. Can't of course. Depression and a sort of homesickness for Singapore. Strange how intensely a fella looks forward to getting back; how for weeks every thought and action pivots upon getting back. And what a fucking let-down it is when he arrives. Then he spends ninety per cent of his time reminiscing and exaggerating what it was like out there.

Wonder what A and G are doing now, Sunday afternoon. They were skint on Friday so they'll probably be lying on their bunks in the barracks reading westerns and playing G's record player . . . or maybe they'll be swimming at the Dieppe pool and moaning because they haven't enough to buy a beer. They'll envy the others who've gone off to exercise in Malaya on HMS *Fearless*. They'll envy me even more flying back here. Hell, they can have it. Wish I was back with them pissing it up in their NAAFI or in the naval base, down round Sembawang or at the Brit Club in Singapore or at one of the hotels preparing for a night in Bugis Street . . . feel lonely as hell when I remember it.

Wonder how T is and K and JW. I've got the green beret and belt and 40 Commando plaque they gave me (a bit wistfully as if I mightn't want them) before I left. They're lying over on the table and comfort me like an old letter or a photograph of someone dead. I'd give up everything, money and all, rather than part with those things they gave me

Wonder what sort of bollocking G collected from his missus when he arrived home after that send-off in the Armada Club; he was legless. Wonder if T has got rid of his dose, and if he has whether he's copped out again Have never seen a fella more dose prone – every week Me, I've never had one; only crabs a couple of times . . .

And the lads in BMH; and the nurses – what a dance we used to lead them. The little Belfast one and the one who got married and B who everyone was after except me and I was the only one who got anywhere. And the bitch of an Irish sister I was always taking the piss out of and Sister R who almost cried when SD and me (I) gave her a box of chocolates the morning we were discharged. Think I'll send her a post card. Better send SD one too. He'll be back in Hong Kong by the time he gets it.

It was good in that ward; we sure had some laughs. I even managed to be half sloshed most of the time. It happened like this: my blood pressure was shooting up and down like a whore's drawers and the lady anaesthetist asked if I knew why. SD was listening so I assumed a modest front and confessed I was an alcoholic. I suffered monumentally when my tap was stopped, I said. The good soul was alarmed and next I knew I was getting a medicinal can of beer hourly. Also my Gurkha neighbour would slip me his daily tot of rum.

I was made up with that hospital . . .

Oh hell, this is more than I care to remember.

Mon. 29th

Misery! Aching all over and sick as a dog.

Feel better in one way, being off the booze, but haven't been able to eat since the plane and my head is drugged with the 'flu.

(Writing this as a therapy – to keep from going mad . . .)

Out this morning. Ten quid for an overcoat then to the Union office, the Shipping Federation, then under the river at the Free Ferry and up to Dreadnought Hospital in Greenwich. Stirring name, Dreadnought. Not like the address of the dentist I was given when I first arrived in Singapore – Dr So-and-So, HMS *Terror*. Wasn't familiar with naval eccentricities then. *Tidepond* was the first Fleet Auxiliary I'd sailed on.

The specialist at Dreadnought was old with that sort of twinkling placidity that makes you feel the person's suffered and learned what life's about and can still smile. He'd worked in Singapore BMH during the war and asked questions on how it stands now. Didn't bother too much about the bone but winked and agreed I should wait a couple of months before working.

Back to the Federation, the Union, the Social Security – endless forms to fill in and me sweating all the while.

Returning to bed and staying there till this fever wears off.

Tues. 30th

Utter gloom!

Wed. 31st

Worse! The cleaning woman a regular Cassandra. She's convinced I'm in my death throes and calls the padre. He's calling a doctor. Long to curl up somewhere warm and quiet and slip off into eternity . . .

Thurs. 1st

Still weak but immensely better. Curious developments. Waiting for phone call from doctor – the old fella at Mass here last Sunday – and if all goes well I'll be living up West . . . in a convent!!!

Fri. 2nd

Going to make a regular thing of this Journal; going to jot it all down; small things, simple things; anything, everything. It certainly looks as though I'll have the time and anyway this room affects me like that . . .

It's large and irregularly shaped with odd corners and caves, and, at the far end where the floor level drops a step, two supporting columns, fluted and handsome and rich. Furniture sparse, but good and solid; a large bed in an alcove, a wardrobe spacious enough to serve as a spare room, an ornate chest of drawers, hard-backed plush-lined chairs and a mahogany table which mesmerises me into sitting down and writing. Combined shower and toilet at the top of a staircase in what appears to be a part of an attic; a strange box-like affair, rather like a tree house.

But the room's dominant feature is the semi-circle of windows, eight of them, trellised-lead diamonds of glass, jutting out like an observation bay almost overhanging the pavement on the corner of the High Street and the lane alongside this building. Reverend Mother says they catch the first sun in the morning as it comes up from Regent's Park and hold it all day until it sinks into Paddington. She says this room has always been the resident man's because it has its own entrance and looks at me fiercely as if every fella is a potential rapist . . . then she breaks into laughter, joyous pealing laughter which embraces you with warm invisible wings . . .

Guess that's half her charm doing that, looking highly efficient one minute and betraying herself with waves of merriment the next. Took my ear-ring out when the doctor drove me here to look over and be looked over but put it back later and forgot to remove it this morning when I arrived with my grip. She spots it right off, claps her hands and sallies into that infectious laugh. 'Ah Keiron' (no Mr Dorrity, nothing formal), 'you are a pirate. I knew you were a sailor but you should have said you were a pirate sailor; that's much more interesting . . .'

Toured the convent and grounds. Larger than it looks from the High Street because this section is the back of the property. Main building a huge white place and faces the park. Whole block squared round with houses belonging to the convent and accommodating the old dears. Area between them a sort of common, an extension of the park, with lawns and flower beds and paths and colourful seats shaded by trees. Walled off section behind this house harbours a rose garden. Exquisitely tended. Bushes are burgeoning into colour and a few blooms exude a perfume which must make the old dears think they're young again.

Looked over boiler. Coal-burning but simple enough. Reverend Mother says it's never caused trouble. Nuns have been stoking it themselves since their old boy died a few weeks ago. Had been with them since before the war.

She started to talk money but I explained how I was already being paid by Federation, Union and Social Security et al. Convent's doing me a favour, I said. If I wasn't here I'd be forking out just to have a roof over my head.

Besides it's only till they get someone permanent . . .

8

Met big black Betty, the cook. Rolling eyes and voice strained through a moonshine still. A power to reckon with. Also several of the nuns – it's difficult to tell one from the other – and one or two of the old dears ambling about.

A happy place. You can breathe contentment in the air like you can breathe the scents in the rose garden. I'll be able to do things here . . .

2000 hrs. Have a telephone, black with number and all. Currently disconnected but Reverend Mother says she'll see to it tomorrow.

Feel like a kid with a birthday. No booze for a week you see. That's the best tonic in the world . . .

Have unpacked solitary grip. Wish I had even half the books I'd collected on the *Tidepond*; I mean, they're no bloody use to the fishes and here are dozens of surfaces crying out to accommodate them . . . yet perhaps better not – it would mean removing all the statues and bleeding hearts and that might offend the nuns.

Have a *Playboy* pin-up but feel she might be persona non grata among the celestial ensemble . . .

Dropped a line to Pete – the bum's not on the phone – on the odd chance that he hasn't shipped out.

Sat. 3rd

So fucking happy want to throw my arms around the world.

In the kitchen the cook, Betty, stands her great black body over me like a storm cloud, forcing me to eat.

Alternating bustle and silence of the convent like a medieval village . . .

This table is a big table and firm and proud. It's stained a deep red, the rich plum colour you'd expect of a wine bottled for centuries. Have moved it nearer the window where I can see the flux of people up and down the High Street. Something hypnotic about watching people walking, the mind spins off into a reverie and reads histories into the woman in moccasins swinging a string bag or the schoolboy spitting into the gutter, a world of tragedy,

9

drama, humour in a sidelong glance or a sudden grimace . . .

Find I develop a sort of tolerance and compassion for humanity (myself included) watching people walking . . .

1300 hrs. Finally through to Eddie's missus. She's had the children in Scotland. Musical voice; soft and springy like butter spreading on fresh bread. Meeting her tomorrow night.

Have made several attempts to write an account of the sinking of the *Tidepond* but it's too soon after the event; I mean I'm too involved. So much happened that night. And all so swiftly. It's a blur in my mind, like a movie you try to remember later, it all comes back to one scene – Eddie laughing like that as we clung to the minesweeper's ladder . . .

Think he'd have kissed me if he'd had the energy . . .

I'll never forget the expression on his face . . .

Never . . .

Want to pay him some sort of tribute. Maybe if I were to set down the story behind his other circumcision (poor old Eddie, he was always getting bits of himself lopped off; it was as if Fate was warning him of his final end), try to get it just as he told me with that blend of innocence and strength he touched everything with . . .

Midnight. Writing for ten hours solid. Exhausting but satisfying, whatever the results:

TWO SWALLOWS

Rumours about Eddie Coulson and why his wife had left him ran pretty wild on that ship. They all concerned sexual in-sufficiency but there were as many whispers as there were whisperers and no one really knew the true story.

The business seemed to worry everyone but Eddie and none was ever man enough to ask him to his face.

I got to know Eddie fairly well that trip. We were on the eight to twelve together and used to sit on the after deck when the watch had finished, sipping beer and looking at the stars and talking. It was on one of these nights he brought the subject up himself, laughed a bit, then, over the beers, this is what he told me . . .

'A few years ago I was shacking up with a kid in the old Seamen's Bethel, West 52nd Street, New York. I was there about a month waiting on a tanker and every day the agent's office said "She'll be in tomorrow Mr Coulson" and that went on for a whole month but it didn't matter because they were paying my wages and the room at the Bethel. I wouldn't have stayed a night in the crummy joint otherwise.

'I'd been flown out from London and the agent took me straight to West 52nd from the airport because it was about 3 o'clock in the morning but he'd left before I'd seen what a dump it was and found I had to share a room. I hate sharing rooms anywhere. I've been on too many ships and in too many missions and doss-houses sharing rooms with geezers whose feet stink and fat old bastards who snore and shit themselves and that. And odd bits of your gear goes missing too, very often.

'Anyway the night I arrived it was too late to do anything about it. The other geezer wasn't making a sound so I left the light off and just bundled into the flea pit and had a kip.

'I woke late the next day and rang the agent's office. They gave me the first of all those "tomorrows" so I went back up the room to fetch my jacket. Thought I might as well mosie around New York seeing as I had a free day. I didn't know the place but I might meet a judy or something and have a good drink. Any place is all right if you meet a judy and have a good drink.

'This kid was in the room; he hadn't been there when I'd gone out. He was lying on his bunk with his hands behind his head staring at the ceiling.

'I didn't pay much attention to him for a start, just said "Hello" or something wondering what a kid was doing in a poxy joint like that and a bit pleased that he didn't look a geezer like the ones I mentioned. He said "Hi!" and I made for the Diner on the corner because I could see one of the old Queens was tied up at Pier 92 and it was common knowledge at sea that the men off those big ships drank in the Diner in those days. There would probably be someone on it I knew.

'Later on I went back up the room for something or other and there was the kid still lying on his bunk looking miserable. "Not going ashore?" I says. "No," he says in that American way that makes one word sound like two so I didn't take any more notice till I was going out and happened to look at him and saw he was crying.

'Well I'm not used to seeing fellas cry. I mean it's a bit weak and even if a fella wanted to cry you'd think he'd wait till no one could see him but this kid was only sixteen or something and he wasn't making any noise at all just these big tears rolling down his cheeks and he looked lonely as hell. I'll tell you I'm not one of your soft bastards but that really got me. I know what it's like to feel lonely like that, don't I though.

' "What's the matter kid?" I says. "Nothing," he says and turns his face away so I wouldn't see him crying. "Come and have a drink." "No thanks." "Well I'll be in the Diner on the corner if you change your mind." So I went back there and drank with the fellas off the Lizzie till she sailed then I was sitting there alone and this same kid came in and sat beside me and asked if I'd buy him a coke. He was sort of shy when he asked as if he'd spent an hour tossing up whether to or not.

'I bought him a coke and asked what ship he was off and he said some Monrovian thing I'd never heard of. Seems he'd joined on the West Coast somewhere and left her in New York a couple of days before then someone had rolled his pay-off. He said he'd had nothing to eat since he'd arrived.

'I knew he wasn't tapping me – I'd have given him the ten dollars anyway – he just wanted to talk to someone I think, being in a strange place not knowing anyone and especially being down. Well he was so grateful for those ten dollars it was worth that much just to see him. He didn't try and refuse them or make me talk him into taking them; he hardly said anything at all really it was just a look about him, made me feel – well I don't know.

'He didn't drink anything, the kid, any beers or spirits I mean, just coke and things like that. Said he was under age and they could nab him if he was found drinking. I sipped slowly as I always do, taking a lot but taking it steady. That's the way I like it.

'In the evening we walked down town around Broadway and into a few of those sleazy dives full of bums and fellas who look at you like you come from outer space somewhere. We went to the pictures too but neither of us liked the show and we walked out before it was over and took the subway down the Village.

'I'll tell you, it was good having the kid around. He was friendly and natural and took everything for what it was. I mean most kids want to do everything all at once. They can't have a drink but they've got to get rotten and they can't have a puff of weed but they want to be junkies, but this kid was different. He was innocent as hell but so calm you'd think he'd done everything there was to do and couldn't be bothered with any of them. It made you feel you wanted to look after him, protect him from all the phoney things people do . . .

'I wish to hell I had've.

'Well like I say we went down the Village that first night and lived it up down there. I like that Village; you can have a good time there and anything goes. We got talking to these couple of nurses (we saw a lot of them after that) and they took us to a few places we wouldn't have found otherwise, good sorts they were and they knew a lot of people. Around two o'clock we went to a party in a basement that was mostly queers and lesbians and nothing to drink but cheap plonk and we only stayed about a half an hour and took a cab back to the Bethel.

'I'd had a lot to drink but I won't make the excuse of saying I was drunk because I wasn't. I was in that state I like to be in when I drink. I don't give a damn for nothing yet everything seems good. You can drink for days like that sometimes if you stick to beer and take it steady but regular, and you never get a lousy hangover.

'Anyway I got into the bunk and the kid turned out the light and got into my bunk alongside me just like that as if it was the most natural thing in the world and said "Might as well, eh!" so I did. "Go easy," he said. "It's my first time." "If it hurts too much tell me and I'll stop."

13

'Next morning when I woke he was in his own bunk reading. I felt a bit of a bastard as I got out to dress and wondered whether I should grunt something, tell him I was drunk or something and smooth it over but when I looked at him he was grinning at me with his head cocked to one side like a spaniel and the grin was fresh and open and I couldn't help but laugh a bit then he laughed too and that was that.

'I rang the agent's office and they said "tomorrow" again so we had another day and then another and then another. As I remember the sun shone every day that month and it was warm. Usually we'd go swimming at Coney Island in the afternoons or maybe stroll through the Bronx Zoo or Central Park or just take a subway anywhere and sit in a bar and I'd drink beer and he'd drink coke though later on he said "to hell with the fuzz" and started drinking beer too and in the evening we'd go to the pictures and finish up in the Village around all those bars and parties down there. Always about three o'clock we'd wind up back at the Bethel and shack up and if ever I felt a twinge of guilt I'd say to myself "Well, I'll be away tomorrow in any case."

'Now on my back on the upper part of my shoulder blades I've got tattoos, two swallows, one each side. I had them done in Rotterdam my first trip to sea about fifteen years ago – I was a kid myself then. They're not bad as tattoos go. The birds are flying inwards and upwards like if they met it would be on the crown of my head and their wings are full of colours. (Yea, OK, I know swallows' wings aren't coloured but that's the way I wanted them done.) I never knew the kid had noticed them but one afternoon in Newark we passed a tattooist's and he said he wanted some done the same as I had so we went in and this old Swedish fella did them, modelling them off mine. They looked good too after a week when the scabs had healed. The colours suited his brown back and when we were shacked up they seemed to me to be flying to nest in that jumbled yellow hair of his.

'Well I won't go on about that month; you can imagine what it was like. The kid never said much, though he was always grinning, and we never mentioned shacking up unless we were in the bunk. But I'll tell you we were happy. Not happy in the same way as a fella is with a judy but more – I don't know – relaxed somehow. Women always want to be emotional and carry on like they're in the pictures. With the kid and me it was different. He knew what I wanted and I knew what he wanted and there was no sloppy mucking about or anything like that. Lust was lust and we didn't try to pretend it was anything else. But we got on great together even apart from that. He had common sense and never got too familiar.

'Actually neither of us spoke much. We never needed to. We seemed to know what the other was thinking all the time. Like, for instance, we were using my money for everything and I knew that hurt him. No man wants to be dependent on someone else for money all the time unless he's a bum. One morning he went out early and came back and said he had a job. Well it didn't matter because I had quite a bit of money and was always expecting him to leave every day and would have seen him OK for a few dollars before I sailed. I was content enough the way things were going but of course I wasn't going to say that. Soon he went out again and came back and said he'd chucked the job in – no explanation, nothing, and I didn't question him. There was no need to.

'I never met anyone else like that, ever.

'One morning very early (we never got up before midday) the agent came round to the Bethel and put me on the shake. The ship was anchored off Long Island. I had to go immediately. I threw my things in a suitcase and left in the agent's car. The kid hadn't woken up . . .

'Well I'd never been back to New York till last trip, on a cargo job. I thought of the kid of course and wondered if he was still around but New York's a big place and it's best to remember things good as they were. He'd probably be a different fella by now and I know I've changed. For one thing I'm married (well, was) with a couple of kids of my own and that makes a man more settled even if he is at sea.

'I wish I'd have thought of that instead of going down the Village that one night we spent there. (You see I wanted to see the kid again even if I told myself different.) I walked around the

15

streets and into some of the bars the kid and I used to go to. It's strange how much a place can change in a few years. I had liked it then. It was new and any minute you expected something exciting to happen. Now it was just drab and sleazy. A lot of the dives had changed their names or disappeared altogether and new places had sprung up somewhere else. There were hardly any of the old faces around either – the same sort of people but different faces and I wondered whether a place changes or whether the change is in the person who sees it.

'I drank here and there, a bit bored, until I ran into Fran, one of the nurses I was telling you about before only she wasn't a nurse any longer. She was doped up to the eyeballs and looked a right slag. We had a drink or two and I asked her if she knew what had happened to the kid. "He's still around," she said vaguely. "He's doing well." I asked where I might find him and she said "Try Leon's off St Mark's." Then she bummed a couple of dollars off me and wandered away.

'This Leon's was down about three flights of stairs and full of smoke and noise and very dark. There were all sorts of junkies and weirdos hanging about and they handed you little plastic flowers as you squeezed your way in. The men had all long hair and beards – I was OK because I'd just grown a bit of a beard myself then – and the women were ghostly and thin as if they'd never seen the sun. Everybody wore freakish clothes but they were decent enough to me when I went in there and I asked this judy where I could get a drink and she took my arm gently and led me through the crowd like I was blind or something. I bought a drink for both of us from this queer barman who fluttered his eyelids at me as he poured them. He had a blouse on, this geezer, one of those ones you can see through and even in that dark place you could make out the bra underneath, a flat looking thing holding up nothing. His hair hung down to his shoulders like a wet rag and he had those plastic flowers stuck in all over it. You could see at a glance that he was a bit of a junkie himself which is OK, his own business, but I didn't go much on the empty self-centred "I'm the Queen of the May" sort of thing he had about him. The judy said "Mother's got it for you, baby." I said "The barman?" "Yea, Leon. If you need anything it all comes from him, even the hard stuff."

'I spent a long time in that place keeping an eye out for the kid and I asked the judy if she knew him but of course she didn't. Trouble was I couldn't remember his name. In fact I don't think I ever knew it.

'The barman had it for me all the time and when the judy disappeared I was on the point of asking if he knew the kid when he said "You wanna smoke honey?" I thought: why not? It was a long time since I'd had a smoke. I followed him through a door and upstairs into a flat that smelt of stale booze and perfume and sat on a couch while he filled the pipe with proper hashish and wriggled his hips and called me "moonchild" and made himself generally familiar.

'The pipe was good. Music came from somewhere and the crummy flat melted into a luxury suite and I didn't give a damn about nothing and even the barman didn't look too bad after he came out of another room wearing a loose dressing-gown. He did a few poses then slumped on to the seat beside me. We puffed the pipe between us and he chatted away with all that talk, trying to impress, but I wasn't listening I felt too good then he started playing about with me and I let him and when the pipe was finished he slid to his knees and went down on me and I just closed my eyes and drifted.

'When I opened my eyes his head was pumping up and down there dreamily and he'd slipped the dressing-gown back over his shoulders like an evening dress and the two swallows tattooed on the upper part of his shoulder blades were flying as if to make to nest in his hair.

'I stretched my hands forward and touched the swallows, smoothing my fingers over them.

' "Kid!" I said.

'He didn't stop what he was doing. He just looked up at me slowly, quiet like, then the whites of his eyes behind the mascara grew wide and bulged out and for an instant I saw a bit of hell there inside his eyes and then he dug his teeth into me and gnawed like a dog twisting it with his mouth and pulling so it seemed he would yank it out by the roots. The pain was terrible and I lashed out at him with my feet and knees and crashed both fists into his face and the side of his head time and time again but he only bit harder and I could feel his sharp teeth sinking into the flesh and the pain was worse than anything you could imagine . . . '

Eddie stopped there and after a long pause shrugged his shoulders to indicate he'd finished.

I grunted noncommittally and continued to study the wake. But it wasn't easy. I was impatient with curiosity and after a silence asked as casually as I could, 'But did it . . . right off?'

Eddie grinned. That much wasn't my business and he didn't plan on telling. 'Well, sort of . . . ' (he affected a droll nonchalance) 'sort of left a nine inch stub . . . '

Sun. 4th

Up at 0630. Raked, stoked and set boiler. Kitchen for cup of tea and Betty descends on me like a mountain. It's Sunday and folk are at Mass mister – in the chapel, up the steps at the end of the corridor, turn right and across the hall. A fool couldn't miss it. I take the hint.

Chapel small but pretty. Walls in contrasting pastels and sheaves of sunlight pouring through windows. I stand among shadows at the back and nuns in their stalls and old dears shuffling in their benches look as if they're caught up in a general apotheosis. I'm the only male there apart from the priest and he looks a sullen fellow. Symbolic rays shy clear of him too.

Eat breakfast and am preached at by Betty. (God in His Goodness decreed, mister . . .) Returning to room am waylaid by old dears who form cordon, three deep, and barrage me with questions. What's my name? Where do I come from? Am I married? Why not? These particulars supplied they take to chin-wagging among themselves . . . then sagacious nods and announcements that I am a good boy and will be a help to the nuns.

Released eventually but not without escort, a tiny Chinese who must be all of eighty and lively as a hen. She totters along at a great pace with arms extended as if to take flight the moment she stops talking. Her room's on the ground floor beneath me and she repeats invitations to come down, come down, come down and drink Guinness with her sometimes. I say I will.

As extra enticement she whispers that she has photographs of her family . . .

Sunday afternoons inch on so slowly . . .

Mon. 5th

Met Mrs Coulson last night; she's nothing like the mousy *hausfrau* I had planned on being avuncular with – a different class altogether.

Can't imagine what she had in common with Eddie, except a natural goodness perhaps.

Actually she intrigued me. I could barely keep my eyes off her then though now my mind refuses to bring her into focus. She keeps disappearing, fading away with that soft laugh of hers, a sort of hayloft giggle, but refined.

She's a lot older than Eddie, in her forties I reckon. Very quiet, very mature; very much the woman. She wore a flimsy flowing thing about her, more like a sari than a dress and her skin was downy and white . . . delicate is a word that springs to mind; fragile; perishable; porcelain. She might have been a bit too much of the hothouse orchid except for a tricky little imp who peeked through her eyes from time to time and puckered her mouth.

I was early and she was late so I'd put away a few pints before we met. It was almost nine and I was thinking she'd been and gone for after all how were we supposed to recognise each other? Was trying to identify all the women in the lounge with the hazy-summer voice I'd heard on the phone when it drifted over my shoulder and suddenly she was there holding my hand in both of hers and beaming.

'Keiron,' she said. 'You *are* Keiron, aren't you? Of course you are. I *feel* it.' She slipped into a chair and smiled as if we'd known each other for years and shared secrets the world could never understand.

I said 'You must be clairvoyant Mrs Coulson.'

She laughed and squeezed my hand. 'Rubbish! The press was full of your pictures. And the box. You're a celebrity Keiron.'

19

'It's all a bit . . . '

'You must call me Agnes. Eddie would want us to be close friends. I'm sure of that.'

I ordered drinks. She lit two cigarettes and handed me one. There was some small talk then she said playfully, 'Do I look so frightful to you Keiron? From your expression one would think I was an apparition.'

Stammered something about being sorry. Hadn't noticed I was staring.

'I'm not the woman you expected, is that it? Not your idea of Eddie's wife?'

'Well, not exactly . . . '

'Tell me everything Keiron, about Eddie I mean. Did he ever speak of me? We'd parted you know (it was all my fault) but the separation was intolerable. We were writing again. He'd more or less promised to stay home after that . . . that confounded ship. Tell me about it. Spare me nothing. I want to know.'

It took me till closing time, supping slowly, to piece together everything I could remember. She sat opposite me with a cigarette in her hand, listening attentively, never interrupting . . .

By the time 'last orders' were called the imp had vanished from her eye. She said, slowly, her chin poised on a ledge made by her fingers, 'It has meant a lot to me Keiron, your contacting me like this . . . an awful lot . . . '

She was crying. She turned aside and fumbled in her bag. 'Silly woman,' she said. 'Come Keiron. Let me drive you home before I make a scene.'

She lives just down from here . . .

Midday. Town this morning. Collected mail redirected from BFPO. Among others a letter from SD now in Hong Kong (addressed to . . . Keiron Dorrity, International Playboy, Sex Symbol, Darling of the Jet Set and Able Bodied Seaman . . .). Meaty scandal when an officer is found turned-in with a steward. S comments: 'The Faculty appear unconcerned by the crimson glare of buggery. What seems to astonish them is that an officer should be on speaking terms with a rating. Presumably if the officer in question could establish that nary a word was spoken . . . '

Bought eight quid's worth of paperbacks.

Looked for and found magazine slanted towards the homo-
erotic. Well got up, good reviews, good illustrations; lousy fiction
– all 'boy-meets-boy, boy-loses-boy, boy-scouts-round-for-
another boy' kind of stuff. Intend to change the names and try
Swallows on the editor.

It's no Chekhov but it's better than anything they've got . . .

Answering letters.

1900 hrs. Working on new project . . . brimming with ideas . . .
Mrs Coulson's for dinner.

Made a cunt of myself again . . .

Polished off a bottle of whisky and got terribly committed . . .

Told her about the Royal What-do-you-call-it Society offering
fifty quid and a medal. She was prouder than if they'd offered it to
her . . . fitting that I should have official recognition, etc . . .

Waxed eloquent . . . 'Listen Mrs Coulson, people help people a
million times a day only no one gets to hear. Because someone
happens to be around with a camera the newspapers make a song
and dance about it so their readers can chalk up another disaster
they've escaped. That makes the world a happier place . . . people
are that much happier, papers are that much happier, photographers
are that much happier – but Eddie had to pay for all that Mrs
Coulson . . . '

'Agnes.'

' . . . Agnes; Eddie and each of those lads who were blown to
pieces that night but Eddie especially because the vultures swooped
up *his* horror with their telescopic lenses and dished it up on the
breakfast tables of the world.'

As I hammed it she sat on the settee with her feet tucked under
her, absorbing every word.

'Do you know where those pictures came from Mrs Coulson?
They weren't taken from the minesweeper; the Admiralty wouldn't
release the pictures taken from the minesweeper. They came from a
liner.

'At dawn an Italian liner hove to for the convenience of her snapshot enthusiasts. Her decks swarmed with happy tourists clicking away getting their money's worth while odd heads and limbs juggled in her wash . . .

'I'll tell you Mrs Coulson I don't want their medal or their bloody money . . . Thirty pieces of silver, that's how I see it . . . thirty pieces of silver . . . '

Woke this morning with a blanket round me and a head like a typhoon. Two little kids staring. Couldn't eat the breakfast she'd cooked. Apologised but she wouldn't hear of it. Was introduced to kids as Daddy's best friend.

(Funny thing is I wrote from Singapore accepting the medal and the money.)

Most of the day working on project though results are pretty meagre. No matter; have made a start and developed ideas.

Balmy evening. A breeze through the window.

Exhausted and content and have no want for anything.

Wed. 7th

NOTES ON PROJECT

Title: Montevideo watching loading of carcasses; half the dockers working about the hatch; rest squatting on deck around brazier grilling steaks; steaks slapped between chunks of bread as big as clogs and eaten with oily salad; the lot is washed down with wine.

Load swinging up from quay breaks loose, tumbling down among them; havoc; pandemonium; foreman, huge Uruguayan with voice like avalanche, thunders for order; crane shackle zooms past his head missing it by inches; pounds fists on forehead and stomps off shouting 'Manicomio, manicomio . . . '

The word glowed and sparkled. It charmed me like a jewel. The more I repeated it the more character it acquired and I thought then: Manicomio – if ever I own a ship that's the name I'll give it . . .

That night I asked a bar girl who was playing with my bollocks what it meant. She told me 'Manicomio! In English you say – what? Madhouse?'

My decision shifted a bit then and *Manicomio* became the title of a book about a ship.

Form: Haven't the experience or discipline to tackle a novel. Will try a sort of montage of stories, poems, paragraphs, etc, all apparently disconnected but reflecting different facets of life in the Merchant Navy.

Something like the *Berlin Stories* or *Last Exit* but looser . . . . . . a cross section of fellas who ship out . . . the same characters appearing without introduction or excuse . . . the effect the life has on them . . . the effect they have on each other . . . the air they breathe . . .

Uppermost in my mind is a character called Dansk. He's a sort of catalyst, influencing the others without changing himself. He doesn't know it but he's a saint. He has no prototype in my experience; he's more of an ideal – the mould of man I'd like to be myself.

A sentence in an autobiography I read suggested him. The writer said: 'As a child, even, I wanted to know someone who saw himself continually in relation to the immensity of time and the universe; who admitted to himself the isolation of his spiritual search and the wholeness of his physical nature.'

He's not real yet; he eludes me. Physically he's nigh perfect though I'd rather this emerged gradually, by inference if possible. As I see him he has corn-blond hair curling over his head; classical features – earthy yet with a strong spiritual glow; skin the colour of eucalyptus bark though strangely transparent like a mask covering another, a more beautiful face; body lithe, hairless, regularly muscular – as if wrung from the imagination of a crazed artist defying nature to produce the perfect form.

It is trying to capture his eyes that Dansk starts to escape me. They are damson blue and dangerously innocent but emotionless in a way I can't find words for.

Burton on the Icelanders: 'A very characteristic feature of the race is the eye, dure and cold as a pebble – the mesmerist would despair at first sight.' Dansk isn't quite so expressionless but he does have that flat impersonal eye peculiar to Northern people.

Perhaps I'm a little scared of him. I know him well yet in a way he's a stranger. I've thought about him a lot at sea, chipping and painting on those long bridge watches when my mind is a ferment of words and places and people pursuing their destinies . . .

Of course he is too perfect; but he is believable because he is perfectly ordinary. He is Christ without Christ's Divinity. And yet he possesses Christ's Divinity because he has accepted the offer of it.

Even his weakness, his epilepsy, is a strength . . . the same strength as Christ's cross . . .

But I'm not ready for Dansk yet. It's his character to slip in unobtrusively and allow his presence to grow.

Working at the moment on a fella called Knocker. Big, moody, animalistic. Attractive in a sullen way. Has never read a book that wasn't a western. Dismisses everything that has no foothold in his working-class norm . . .

Walked Regent's Park with Mrs Coulson and the children. By the lake she says airily, 'When Eddie made love he took me to another planet, no winds, no weather . . . I was perfectly secure . . .'

Thurs. 8th

Will never tire of this room. It's like a stage with three sets – a Greek temple, a baronial hall, and the poop cabin of a sailing-ship – and the stagehands don't know which to dismantle because they haven't been told what's playing next . . .

Crossed to the local last night and fetched ale back. Sat here reading and supping and gazing out the window. Splendid tranquillity.

Writing a bit but too lazy mostly.

Movies with Mrs Coulson. Utter nonsense. Fell asleep.

Fri. 9th

There's a peace in this convent, a serenity which rises out of the ground and seeps through the walls to wrap itself around you wherever you go. Perhaps it's simply the novelty yet I feel the women experience it too, no matter how long they've been here. It's almost tangible on the faces and in the demeanour of the nuns and even the most crotchety old ladies appear to complain but superficially, by habit, as if their inner selves were anchored safely in some harbour no matter what winds blew.

In the rose garden at lunch-time I get to thinking about this inner selves bit, but introspection is so frustrating . . .

When I try to look at myself objectively I get all tied up in knots . . .

I can dig no deeper than the outer layers of skin . . .

Beyond that, vague darkness . . . amorphous confusion . . .

1600 hrs. Joy! Telephone connected.
An hour talking to Mrs Coulson.
Who else do I know to ring?

Sat. 10th

Speedy response for *Swallows*. Editor (Yoop van Leer) delighted. Editor's policy to publish short biographical note on writers; could I send personal data and, if possible, photographs. Also phone number if I would like to discuss further articles . . .

Chuffed . . .

All photos went down with the *Tidepond*. Will have to send the one the Bootnecks took. My arm's in a sling and I'm trying to work a tiller.

Sun. 11th

At Agnes Coulson's last night. Drunk again. She never seems to get pissed herself.

Up early though. Boiler, Mass, bite of breakfast and I settle to the desk. But my mind is off grazing in other fields and gallops away playfully when I attempt to harness it. So I turn in again.

Doze a while and next I know I've a terrible hard on; one of those adamant sexless ones, as angry as a mad bull and as intractable. Hero writhes and twists trying to find a position where it won't be felt but might as well be wrestling with an anaconda.

Throw the sheets back and am half way through wanking when a knock sounds on the door.

Pull up the sheets. Must be a nun. Or one of the old dears. Damn thing'll stick out a mile behind a towel or a pair of trousers. (I boast!) Nothing for it but to stay in bed. Try to look as if I've just woken and call 'Come in'.

It's the sullen priest though he's not as sullen as I'd supposed. Says his name is Father Michael.

Says he's making himself known.

He's sorry if he's woken me; he'd thought I was up and about . . .

I say I had been but I'd returned to bed.

I say I wasn't feeling myself. (Priceless gem of wit – totally lost!)

He shows professional concern.

I say it's nothing; it will pass.

An awkward silence.

I sit up by way of making him feel welcome. He studies my body disconcertingly. The sheet laps my loins and I look to see if the extension's showing. It isn't, but the tattoo is, and it's pretty obvious where it leads to.

I say, 'Oh – tattoo!' and hazard a laugh.

He glances at my books and asks if he might look through them. He fingers the odd copy but his eyes are on my body in the mirror. At length he says, 'An interesting collection. They say you can judge a man by the books he reads.' He is holding *Querelle of Brest*.

He smiles, suddenly, warmly. 'Be wary of those nuns.' His voice is clipped and humorous. 'They're dangerous. They make ghastly saints out of interesting sinners.'

He spots my liquor stock on the table and remarks cheerily 'Ah, a drunkard! Good! We'll get drunk together sometimes. Talk about your books, eh?'

He leaves abruptly.

Either he's got high tension nerves disciplined to a sober front or he's naturally dispassionate and disguises the fact with a show of sanguinity.

He's all right as a geezer though; I feel I like him.

When he's gone I light a cigarette and muse a while. Then I finish off the wank because it's gotten into the blood . . .

1500 hrs. Raining.

Sunday afternoons weighty and interminable . . . weekly glimpse of eternity . . .

Where can one go to escape the gloom of a rainy Sunday . . . ?

Mon. 12th

1600 hrs. Ambled among shops browsing in the sun. A vast pleasantness gazing into shop windows with the sun shining and money jangling in your pocket.

Bought a glass mermaid shot through with rainbows like the marbles we used to play with as kids. She lies on a metal rock and has no practical function except perhaps as a paperweight. Cost four quid and is well worth it.

Also bought shirt, shoes and cashmere jumper as replacement for those lying on ocean bed. Rarely buy gear and when I do it's with a sense of guilt. I mean it's cutting into good drinking money. Besides I've no dress sense. Can recognise it in other people but settle for conventional cuts in plain grey and fawns and blues myself. Who needs sartorial style anyway when nine times out of ten shore rig is flip-flops, jeans and a gungey T-shirt?

A lot of work. Knocker is taking good shape.

Strange preoccupation with marriage among the aged.

Ambushed by old dears on my way back from evening meal. Are you married? Have you got a girl? Fine boy like you should get himself a girl. (It's their woodpecker theme.) Never, says I, I'll never step into that trap. Nonsense, wagging their heads and laughing wisely, you're young yet, you'll get caught, before you know it some pretty little thing'll sweep you off your feet, wait and see.

Guess they're right to taunt the convinced bachelor but, hell, I just don't like most women too much . . . unless they worship me, and then it's no more than a grudging admiration for their taste . . .

Tues. 13th

0300 hrs. Just back from Agnes's.

We shacked up. It was inevitable I guess.

We were lying on the floor reading poetry and it just happened. No hang-ups, no regrets; not much lust even . . .

Feel suspended in a warm dark place . . .

Don't particularly want to talk about it right now . . .

0830. Hour on boiler to justify being here. Got pressure steady and swept out entire place. Burnt old newspapers and accumulated rubbish. Salvaged copy of *HMS Ulysses* – opening pages nigh perfect.

Like a chimney-sweep when finished but detoured round convent and walked the side lane to avoid old Chinese Mrs Grey, who hovered on the direct path. She proved the better strategist though because she was waiting in the rose garden. Didn't give her an opening; just waved cheerily and ran up the stairs. Close shave!

*

1230. Forewent breakfast to avoid Mrs Grey.

Keen for work today. Writing all morning. Wish I could stick to the one thing though. Keep flitting from *Camaraderie* to long-winded poems to vague ideas to this Journal . . . too much enthusiasm . . .

1400. Think Betty resents strangers. She's purifying me in a crucible before admitting me to the sanctum of her approval. Her favourite fire is a sort of inquisition, a test for orthodoxy. Today it's de pill. 'De pill's wrong. De Pope's right 'bout dat. OK mister?'

Mrs Grey on watch in the rose garden. She kneels on a dirty silk cushion trowelling the soil at the feet of a statue. One hand clutches at the Virgin for balance. Seeing me she brandishes the trowel dangerously and stumbles to her feet. 'Oh, you're just the one I've been looking for,' she cries in her old-door-on-rusty-hinges voice, and adds ominously 'I never know where to lay my hands on you.' She does an intricate Siamese dance with her arms outstretched, her ancient Chinese eyes squeezed tight and her wizened head swivelling about on her neck as if on a base of ball bearings. 'Wherever have you been?'

'In my room mostly, Mrs Grey.'

'Oh, oh! That's not healthy. Young men should be out enjoying themselves.'

She performs a few more votive dances then standing shakily akimbo says 'I need you to move my bed. It's all wrong. It needs moving.' She leads the way like a semaphorist with piles.

Bed moving proves inartistic. Furniture shifted from port to starboard simply gives the impression of walking in the wrong door. However, before the job's completed she has set Guinness on a table and is insisting that I drink.

Photograph album materialises, as if by accident, and she leafs through it with practised commentary . . . ancient brown prints of her in infancy, taken in China twenty years before the Boxer Rebellion; prim poses at a school conducted by French nuns in Saigon; more in Macao where she married her first Frenchman. Most Far East countries represented and, from what I can make out, at least six husbands – all either French or English because, she confides, she only speaks the two languages . . .

Shots too on the slopes of Victoria in Hong Kong where, she tells me with animation, her eldest daughter lives, adding vaguely 'if she's still alive'.

Pictures telling of social life in London and Paris between the wars, of affluence and good living in fine houses, innumerable relations, influential friends until the history winds up here at the convent.

After four Guinnesses and a scotch I'm permitted to leave. Am halfway into the rose garden when she calls 'I'm ninety you know; ninety next month. All the family is coming for my birthday. First time all the family will have been together.

'In Mons you know, in Belgium, I have three great great grandchildren – three *great great* grandchildren. Would you believe that? Yes, and they're getting in touch with my daughter in Hong Kong; she'll be over too – if she's still there . . .

'Bye bye . . .'

Told Father Michael about it. His comment was 'She's randy that one . . .'

Hell, at ninety!!!

Going into the West End on the piss tonight – give Agnes the miss. Does women no good to let them think you need them.

Wed. 14th

1930 hrs. First call. Pete. Hasn't shipped out for six months. Is in business flogging eggs . . . and odds and ends 'wot 'ave fell awf backs uv lorries'.

Coming round tomorrow evening.

He's my best mate, Pete . . .

Thurs. 15th

Dissatisfaction with literary efforts. Chief problem is verbosity.

CAMARADERIE

Close by the main docks either side of the tram lines leading into Bremen is a nest of seamen's bars which the Germans call Die Küste though it is better known among our lads as Golden City – not that it's a Babylon of excitement or anything like that but because Golden City is the name of the oldest, biggest, sleaziest and best known bar in the quarter.

On subsequent trips when Knocker wound up there he would remember the fella Gunter and tell the crowd he was with how he'd gone on the booze with a kinky Kraut who'd fallen in love with him and tried to do 'isself in. With a few fabrications the story was always good for a laugh until eventually Knocker believed the concocted version himself and forgot what had actually taken place . . .

The night he'd met him Knocker had wandered ashore early to nose around and get a good skin-full against the next day's sailing. The cold coiled round and clung to him as he stepped from the tram and he wished he'd worn more than dungey jacket and jeans.

He walked, shivering, into the nearest bar, sat at a table and called for beer. In spite of the cold he felt good. He had all night to get rotten in and no one to worry about but Number One.

He might even get a bang off . . .

He didn't take much notice when a voice next to him said 'Hey, you are Englander? I speak little English you know.' He just mumbled 'Big deal' and didn't look at the speaker. He thought the fella was bumming booze. That was the trouble with honky tonk bars – down to the head with bums. He leaned towards the juke-box and strummed to the rhythm.

'In Deutschland we learn English in school. Hey, you speak Deutsch, yes?'

'No!' Piss off and bum somewhere else.

The barmaid placed a bottle of Haake-Beck on the table and Knocker dug for money. The German said 'Hey, no sweat. You take this from me, yes please.' And he handed the girl a note.

31

Knocker shrugged. He wasn't enthusiastic.

'I am in Par once four mud. Hey, you from Par?'

'London,' he muttered.

'I like very much to go to London. Piccadilly Circus, yes? Buckingham Palace?'

Knocker took a long slow draught. A blues singer poured her soul out of the juke-box. A drunk woman shuffled and swayed to the beat. He thought: What's this geezer after? Could be he's a pimp; or maybe just a con. Perhaps he's fruit? No, he's not fruit. You can nearly always tell. Sort of telepathy.

Knocker turned and looked at him. He was young, about eighteen or nineteen, with a fresh and pleasant face which alternated between youthful toughness and boyish prettiness neither of which disguised the eager sincereity of his expression.

But Knocker noted little of this. He thought simply: A geezer shouldn't have hair that colour – but of course he was a Hun.

Knocker looked away. 'Yea. Big place London.' He finished his glass and called the barmaid. As an afterthought he said to the German 'Do you . . . um . . . another beer?' and without waiting for an answer ordered two more.

When the drinks came the German said 'My name is Gunter,' and half his face flashed a grin. One eye almost winked and a corner of his mouth darted mischievously towards a dimple.

'Yeah! No kiddin'?'

'Cheerio, my friend.'

Knocker raised his glass. 'You shootin' orf then . . . ?'

Gunter said his home was in Stuttgart (Knocker had never heard of it) and that he was a deck-hand with Norddeutscher Lloyd. 'Mine is a good ship,' he told Knocker, 'but maybe soon I have more – no – another. Hey, maybe I on your ship, yes? Then I learn English good and we drink much beer.'

The drunk woman threw her arms around the juke-box and vomited copiously. Gunter said 'Come, we drink in more bar, eh? This place shitzenhausen . . . '

He might know some decent dives, whatever his game was – what the hell!

They caroused systematically from bar to bar all along The Coast. Some bars showed movies on a screen hung over the windows, old Chaplin silents and mildly erotic strips – for the real sexy work-out you had to go into a backroom where a beer cost four marks. Other bars made do with a piano or an accordion player. All provided some attraction and a few served food but the only thing that really mattered was the booze.

As the evening advanced the crowds in the bars and on the streets thickened. Men stepped down off the ships for a run ashore and the girls who slept all day came out from the houses to meet them.

By midnight The Coast was jumping.

In the 'Crocodil' a street-girl whom Gunter seemed to know sat with them and they bought her drinks. Knocker looked her over carefully. A bit on the heavy side but smashin' Bristols – if they were all hers. And a dead peachy mouth. He wondered idly how much for a short time but she spoke no English and ignored him anyhow. After several rounds he leaned across the table and said to Gunter 'If you fancy your 'ole mate, don' mind me'.

'What this mean – fancy yirole?'

'If you wanta bang off, you know . . . ?' He made circular motions with his hand as if it would rake in an appropriate word from the air. None forthcoming he used the only one he knew.

Gunter laughed and translated for the girl who knew *that* much English anyway. To Knocker he said 'No, no my friend, you are thinking wrong. Not for me this woman . . . '

So he is fruit, thought Knocker.

Then, with sudden animation Gunter burst out 'Hey, you would like her, yes? She give you good time. House quick from here.'

Knocker looked her over again. He wasn't really all that interested. You thought a lot about it at sea and in the mornings but the chase was half of it. When it was wrapped up for you like meat at a butcher's it wasn't the same. It lost the magic. Still . . . 'How much?' he asked.

'I think maybe forty marks. Here, I buy for you, no sweat.' He drew a fistful of crumpled notes from a top pocket.

Knocker wasn't too anxious. But he wasn't going to say no. A grind was a grind and she had smashin' Bristols. His thoughts fanned the flame in his flesh. He half smiled, half shrugged and said 'Well, if you put it like that . . . ' but negotiations were interrupted by the girl.

She stood abruptly, sneered with contempt and spat 'Englander bastard!'

Knocker threw her a Victory as she stomped out of the bar.

Gunter apologised – profusely. 'I get for you one more soon. You leave to me, yes?'

'Don't bovver mate; lost me appetite.'

Gunter said 'Girls good, but not from street . . . '

Perhaps he wasn't fruit after all.

It was still cold on the street but by their third time round The Coast Knocker didn't feel it any more. They were somewhere between the St Pauli Bar and the Blue Lamp, arms around one another's shoulders and clutching bottles singing a bilingual version of 'Dinah Dinah, Show Us A Leg' when they met a crowd from Gunter's ship who hailed him and they all went into the Blue Lamp together.

They sat at a table and talked and laughed loudly and pinched the bottom of the girl who brought the drinks. Knocker (for whom wogs usually began at Calais) was in a right rare mood and conceded that they were a decent lot of Huns.

They slapped him on the back and insisted he drink Schnapps. In another bar he announced that he was prepared to forget the war. They sang 'God Save the Queen' and, later, 'Deutschland Über Alles'.

On the street between bars a bearded Pole who had been particularly friendly nudged Knocker's arm, cocked his head in Gunter's direction and said slyly 'You are all right for tonight, eh!'

So the kid was fruit.

Somehow they lost the others and were back in the St Pauli. Knocker's elbow upset a woman's glass and Gunter bought her another. The drink had stained her dress and she wailed about it all through the blue movie. Knocker got his hand a good way up her thigh and she threatened to stub her cigarette on it. Knocker laughed and defied her and the burn didn't half sting for a while – mad cow!

The bearded Pole sat in the Elegant Bar alone. Gunter was anxious to avoid him. Knocker wondered why until next door Gunter explained. 'That man he never leave me alone. Always he want to make me like a woman, you know? Many times we fight. Oh, he very crazy man . . . ' Gunter was bent over his glass, fingering it, shaking his head. Suddenly he laughed. 'Hey, you know, one day I make joke with him. I say "Give me one bottle whisky and come to cabin . . . late at night". He give me whisky and I take to my cabin and my friends we become drunk. Oh, next day he very angry, yes . . . '

He wasn't fruit.

They were still jostled on the streets but the crowds had begun to thin out. At a stall they bought sausages over a foot long and a miserable looking geezer tried to sell them a dog. Gunter slipped the man a couple of marks and told Knocker he was on the needle and had probably stolen the dog. Knocker said 'Bleedin' bum! You shouldn't have given 'im nuffin'' but it was only his way of talking and he couldn't care less really.

In the Golden City Gunter, who had been gazing at Knocker for some time (Knocker thought the booze was telling and that Gunter was trying to focus) grasped his arm and said with intensity 'Hey, you are my friend, yes. You are my friend for always.'

Knocker said 'Sure fing, you're a decent geezer. 'Ere, shake on it.'

Gunter shook Knocker's hand with both of his and leaned across and kissed him on the cheek.

He was fruit.

Well, what the hell; Knocker didn't give a monkey's.

Gunter was looking at him with admiration and something else and Knocker felt good and pretty important and grinned at him as he drank his beer.

Just then a fight broke out at the bar. A German hit a coloured fellow who retaliated with a vicious swing and the German toppled back on top of Gunter. Gunter heaved him off and the German lashed back and Gunter sprang at him like a tiger, flooring him then punching him five, six, seven times in the face

35

and those around could hear bones and teeth cracking. The coloured fellow and his friend hauled him off but he turned on them and they hit back so Knocker (who could use himself) leapt into the battle and dealt a few blows here and there and collected a heavy one on the ear before he managed to drag Gunter out the door and into the safety of a quiet bar.

There was no damage done, no blood, but Gunter was badly shaken. He laughed and sobbed alternately and insisted that Knocker was his best friend because he had fought when Gunter had fought and saved him from the niggers who would have killed him and he promised that one day he would show Knocker that he meant it when he said he was his best friend and Knocker wouldn't be sorry . . .

They drank in the bar for more than an hour, Gunter talking, talking, and Knocker listening, sometimes to Gunter, sometimes to his own thoughts, buoyed up by alcoholic euphoria and a sense of pride in his own acknowledged virility.

Once or twice as he spoke of friendship Gunter placed his hand on Knocker's, right there in the bar, in front of everybody but Knocker didn't give a damn. He was a good kid, even if he was fruit and he, Knocker, would personally kick the head in of anyone who wanted to take the piss.

The bearded Pole entered the bar but he was drunk and didn't recognise them as his eyes prowled among the few remaining drinkers. Gunter said 'Let us move from here' and they went out into the street.

It was after four o'clock and The Coast was folding up. An early morning mist hung around street lamps and lighted doorways making them like shrouded corpses. Most of the bars had closed or were closing and cleaners were already at work. The girls on the street corners were calling it a night, ambling home slowly, reluctantly, searching among the few remaining seamen straggling back to their ships for a last minute score – or perhaps even, in desperation, for a lover.

A slowly moving truck sprayed water on the streets which washed all the litter into the gutter. It was as if daylight must never suspect the night habits of people.

The sudden sharp cold hit Knocker and all at once he felt the weight of his drunkenness and his limbs grumbled for sleep. He said 'I best be headin' back; gotta turn-to in a couple of hours' wondering if Gunter was going to chat him up and what he'd do if he did. He didn't want to offend Gunter because he was a bloody good kid, a great kid really, but at the same time he didn't want him to go thinking . . .

Gunter said 'Me also, I must work one hour from now. We have last drink in Golden City, yes?'

Neither the coloured fellows nor the German were in the bar. A handful of people, less conspicuous than their shadows, sat at tables and near the till a woman dozed. She started when they asked for beer but smiled approvingly when she recognised Gunter. She spoke to him in German and wouldn't let him pay for the drinks. At the table he told Knocker that the German he had laid out had been taken to hospital and that the barmaids were pleased because he was always causing trouble. He said 'Maybe it is me in the hospital if you not fight with me. You are my friend.'

Knocker was very tired. If he didn't leave soon he might flake out and miss the ship. 'Forget it,' he said.

Gunter took a sip of his beer. He leaned across the table and grasped Knocker's hand once more. He didn't seem drunk at all and sincerity burned on his handsome, pretty face. 'Always I look for a real friend. You are my friend, my real friend. No matter for other people. I am for you, yes?'

There was no doubt he was fruit.

Knocker finished his glass. 'Sure fing mate. Listen, I gotta get movin'. Might see you next time eh!'

Gunter was reluctant to release his hand. He said nothing but stared at him frankly, pleadingly, as a prisoner cemented in his dungeon stares through the small square in the wall at the other prisoner across the flags.

Knocker squirmed. His privacy was being invaded; Gunter's look touched a nerve. He drew his hand away and with more venom than he intended said 'Wot the 'ell do you want orf me mate, wot you after? Sex – that's it isn't it? You're fruit an' you're lookin' for a geezer. I sus the . . . WILL YOU QUIT GAPIN' AT ME LIKE THAT FOR CHRIS' SAKE.'

Gunter didn't appear to understand but he grinned as if he'd agree with anything Knocker said.

Knocker rose to go. 'Sorry mate, I didn't mean that. I'm knackered. See you round.'

Gunter smiled, happy suddenly, excited. 'Hey, I have idea. One moment please.' He called to the barmaid speaking to her rapidly. She raised an eyebrow, shrugged, and fetching a whittle knife from the kitchen behind her flung it across the bar. The edge of the knife glinted hard steel as Gunter ran his thumb along the surface. He said 'I read in book one time where friends become brothers of blood. They cut here and mix blood so always they are brothers. We cut, yes?'

Knocker's frown hovered between surprise and disgust. 'Don't be daft mate, that's daft.'

Gunter tugged at his sleeve and laid his hand palm up on the table. He raised the knife and slashed. As Knocker grabbed for it the knife nicked his thumb and his hand caught the fountain of blood spurting out of the wrist. The woman screamed and ran into the street shouting for police. Gunter laid the knife on the table and pushed it towards Knocker.

Knocker backed into the middle of the room and stood there, mesmerised by the blood dripping from his hand, the blood in thick scarlet pools on the table, and the blood flowing gently from Gunter's wrist into the hand stretched out like a beggar's toward him.

The police did a lot of talking though everything was in a kind of cloud to Knocker. They seemed to be blaming him for the blood but he didn't understand the language so he couldn't tell why. When the woman swabbed Gunter's wound it was found to be very small (the cut on Knocker's thumb was bigger) when the blood ceased to flow. She bandaged the wrist and crooned into his hair. Later the police went and Gunter just sat at the table with his hand out still looking at Knocker like that, waiting.

Knocker left the bar.

In the taxi he felt angry and tired and his head throbbed and tried to push his eyes out every time he moved it. He felt dissatisfied as if something had escaped him, as if he hadn't really been in command of the situation . . . but hell, it had all happened so quickly. He told himself that the kid must have been a nutter anyway.

But he wasn't quite convinced so he told himself again.

Over and over again he told himself. 'Bloody nutter,' was his formula. 'Why do I get tangled up with nutters every time?'

1930. Pete due any time. Toured locals last night in case we drink round here. Nothing much. One called the Welbeck is pretty lively.

There's a queer bar just off the High Street. Typical. Had them eating out of my hand there last night.

16th Friday or something

Address of party from coloured people in Welbeck. Miles away – south of the river. Covens of Africans squat around door. Slightly sinister so we smile bravely and walk among them and sit down. After initial suspicion they prove friendly. Won't let us go to top floor in case we're filled in. Dispatch boy who returns with attractive black girl called Mary. 'Hey, yous Tessie's friends. Up dis way.' All black girls there but some of the fellas European. Cheap place, except for booze. One wall wire-netting. Broken chairs, stinking piss house, wonderfully friendly. Big Nigerian lad tells of white fella being carted off earlier in evening for interfering with small boy. Later he says he got the story wrong – the white fella paid a black fella to get stuck up him. I say 'Thought it was legal?'

'In de street man? Dey don't even do dat in Dakar.'

Girl called Mona on my knee, kissing, dancing. Always about to go to bed but doesn't move. Around 0400 she says 'You come sleep with Mona – must leave trousers on.' Delightful arrangement and off we stumble to a downstairs room where she washes my feet in a bucket and dries them with a pink towel. Removes my shirt. Lie on bed which takes up most of room – also wardrobe, table with mirror, photographs and sugary print of crucifixion. Try, but can't get her to come across. Sleep.

Wake entwined. Black skin of her neck and black skin of her cheek glow with velvet loveliness. Breasts exquisitely soft beneath shift. I smoke. Fondle and admire her in half sleep. Trek through corridor of house talking to happy people outside doors. Piss in bucket in back yard. Muzzled by kids who haven't learned to walk yet. Back to Mona then up to bar. People speak. Some (suppose I must have met them) shake hands. Pete arrives with tongue in Mary's ear. Beer. Girls. Music. High time. Go and wake Mona by shaking money in her face. She comes to bar. Drink. Beautiful Nigerian lad called Bill with three-inch thumbnail. Later Pete, Bill, Mary, Mona and me to some bird's gaff where we all get blasted on weed. Couple up and exit for bang-off. I with Mona (I think). Great but slow coming. Later back to bar. The whole world there. High as a cloud. Just back. Boiler out. Pete flaked. Looks dead but happy.

Me? . . . brother I'm floating . . .

Love Nigeria!

Woken by phone. Feel pretty good considering.

Meeting *Ganymede* editor *Sunday* night. Hardly business-like. What gives? (Bet he's going to chat me up.)

Pete stumbling about moaning because he's missed his weekend egg delivery.

Tough baby!

He seems more worried about it than he is about his bird being pregnant.

Party in his Walthamstow local tomorrow so I'm taking it easy tonight. Movie or quiet drink or something.

Sat. 17th

True to resolution last night, no booze. Tea and sympathy with Agnes. Her body soft and comfortable. She uses it in every possible way to please yet retains a maidenly modesty. Calls me her young hero as when I've come my dust. (Hope I didn't catch a dose off that black piece.)

Agnes pretty chuffed with me I reckon. I'd feel a lot easier if she'd stop comparing me with Eddie though.

Wonder if she knows the full story of New York . . .

Twilight lies low and lazy over London. Feel I'm in for a good night.

Sun. 18th

Pete greets Penny with ''Ad a dream 'bout you last night' – Penny a shrubbery of smiles; Pete's tone drops – 'Dirty girl!'

Fellas all put three quid in a kitty and that sees the night through. You drink whatever you want. So do the bloody females . . .

Governor shuts the door at closing time and pulls the curtains – token precaution because the fella whose coming-of-age we celebrate is a local copper's son, a hefty ginger lout who says nothing till midnight then, on thawing, trumpets his prowess as a dart player. Can hold his own with the best in the 'Stow. Is last seen spewing up in the piss-house. Someone tells me he's always in institutions for nicking women's underwear.

'Stow people much more my sort than those round here. You don't have to put on side like people do in NW8 – and if you do you're told soon enough.

Pete's bird (I forget her name) a honey. Too good for him I tell her. Cuddly face like a panda and very black eyes, wide with wonder.

She says 'I'm pleased to meet you at last; I've read everything you've written.'

Pete (who dismisses my literary aspirations as crap) winces, then cuts in, 'Wot! You been doin' the piss-'ouses fen?'

She ignores him, rather prettily. 'He shows me all your things and I'm not ashamed to say I'm a great admirer of yours.'

'Thanks.' I'm astonishingly modest.

'I cried when I read your poem.'

Pete says 'I don't fuckin' wonder'.

'I thought it was harrowing and wonderfully graphic.'

'Pornographic . . . ' from Pete.

'Which one?' I ask as if I've written volumes of harrowing, wonderfully graphic poems.

Fred says:

> 'We went for a ride in a chuff-chuff,
> There was only room to stand;
> A small boy offered me his seat
> And I grasped it with my hand.'

Fred's a friend of Pete's. Used to be a steward with P & O. Has got the slanted sort of oriental eyes of a wide-boy and a wry sense of humour. You can read his history in the cut of his suit. I like him.

His wife easily the best looking woman in the bar. Sweet disposition. Don't think she's a local girl. On the side I say to Pete 'How did Fred get himself a classy bird like that?'

'S'pose 'e 'ad to settle for 'er. I mean wiv a bleedin' boat race like vat 'e couldn't expect a decent geezer, could 'e?'

Fred's sister's voice like an alley cat being raped.

Many people. Couple whose daughter's making films in Italy and a fella who did National Service in Singapore.

Get stuck necking with Penny in a corner. 'I'm not like I was, Keiron, I've changed you know . . . ' Great! Best news in a long while.

'I've got a steady boy friend now; he's in the navy . . . ' Sounds cute. Get your hand back underneath my shirt.

'If you think things are going to be as they were you might as well know I'm not that sort of girl any more . . . ' OK. That's a bastard of a zip on the back of your dress.

Later in her flat in Stratford we drink coffee and discuss (with remarkable objectivity) the pros and cons of shacking up again . . .

'Gary loves me Keiron and Gary's going to marry me; he's got a prick like a pillar-box and he doesn't sleep with queers . . . '

Used to knock around together when I was doing six-week trips on the 'A' boats till she found out I was having it away with one of the queens aboard. Told her myself as it happens, mentioned it in passing. Thought she knew. Everybody else did.

She went spare at the time, threw wobblers all over the place, got neurotic and pestered everyone we knew with her reflections on fidelity. Avoided her for days then the night we were due to sail all the ship's crowd were drinking in the 'Steps' down Customs-house and in she stalks doing a Sarah Bernhardt. We would remain friends, she said in her *refeened* stage whisper, but she couldn't bring herself to continue intimacy with a man who had slept with other men. (She had a lousy script-writer.) Told her she'd have a bloody hard job finding a fella then, especially with her appetite ... but it didn't sink in ...

All patched up this morning though. We were both shattered *and* we had to share the bed with her flat-mate but fucking rhapsody it was just the same. She's an idiot but I can relax with her.

Fell asleep in cab. Boiler. Sister G on Common helping old dear on crutches. I say 'Good morning'. She smiles beatifically and answers soundlessly, mouthing words as if reluctant to disturb the sheer silence of a new day. Then, as if something important had suddenly sprung to mind she whispers 'Oh, Keiron. It's not Sunday Mass this morning by the way. It's Saint Someoneorother, our Holy Foundress.' Oooh and nod as if I've been worried sick about it for days. Force myself into chapel where I spend a wretched hour trying to keep awake.

All day, blessedly, sleep.

Meeting *Ganymede* editor tonight in local queer bar; taking Agnes as counterbalance.

Mon. 19th

0400 hrs. Back from Agnes's.

Rapport with the kids and later, after we'd tucked them in, grand passion. Pretty good having it laid on whenever you want it, though I've really had too much lately.

Lying there sated, with her head on my belly, she says 'Keiron, I must be the happiest female on the planet ... ' Then ' ... and women want to be liberated . . . Whatever from? This? Male dominance? . . . We'd be spineless . . . freaks! Oh darling here's one that doesn't – dominate me all you want, only let me adore you . . . '

Little snotty-nosed Dorrity who used to eat other kids' apple cores elevated to worshipful object . . .

Feel kind of mellow and floating.

1100. Met editor last night. Yoop van Leer. Dutch. About thirty. Right decent geezer but a weakness somewhere. Don't reckon he's bent though. Probably in it for the money. Apart from the magazine there's a chain of clubs and a hotel and I don't know what else.

Big business, buggery . . .

He wants more stories but you can't just sit down and write a story. It's got to come when it's ready, like rain.

His side-kick's a snidey bastard – 'worst by-product of the English public school system' as Alistair Maclean says of one of his characters. His name's Eugene.

We weren't half treated well though. Luckily *Swallows* wasn't mentioned in any detail or Agnes might have got suspicious. Yoop did say 'Was it a true story?' so I said 'Hell no!' to dismiss the subject.

The peacock-faced Eugene said prissily 'I suppose you've checked if it's biologically feasible . . . '

Not much more than an hour with them; think they just wanted to look me over.

Tues. 20th

Tempted to give this notebook up . . . time stolen from *Manicomio*, etc but sixth sense tells me it's a benefit, a discipline.

Trying too hard to be the writer. Immature. Many passages contrived. Volatile. Imitative. Like my handwriting where the style of one line is seldom uniform with the next . . . like my living too, I guess . . .

If I could be myself . . . whatever that is . . .

Grappling with *Manicomio* all morning. Dansk won't speak. Wrote his dialogue arbitrarily to tackle later. You know, I think I'm too involved with him emotionally. Wish I could be more objective, more clinical.

1630. Fix toilet window in main building. Measure it up, walk to Swiss Cottage to buy glass and putty, come back and do job neatly with table-knife. Am beaming with justifiable pride when quaint stalk of antiquity limps in, sees me, abandons stick and flees screaming into the nunnery. I retreat with dignity but all the long length of the corridor shocked curious heads peer out from behind doorways and outraged matrons slink in terror against walls.

Reverend Mother thinks it hugely funny and wishes she'd been there.

Pete rings . . . he still entertains a hangover from Saturday.

Agnes's again. Life falling into a routine pattern.

Wed. 21st

Whisky with Agnes.

Drinking too much too often.

Working on poems for *Manicomio*.

Thurs. 22nd

Wrong about Yoop. He sucked me off in the taxi.

Pissing down outside, and chilly. Christmassy. How's this for *Manicomio*?

SAILOR'S CHRISTMAS

All right sweetheart? Merry Christmas and all that!
Wonder what you're doing now! Still at dinner I guess
With paper hats and bon-bons and steaming pud. OK is it?

45

Has your Old Dear come? How does Danny like what Santa
　　brought?
Bet he's chuffed to find the puppy *and* the train. What's he say?
What's he plan to name it? Does he ask where I am at all?
Hell, Susan, I wish I was home right now.

Merry Christmas! That's a laugh. No one on here dares say
　　'Merry Christmas'.
We scrunch through ice as thick as that concrete by the roses
(Did you sack the roots?), the heating's off and water's frozen in
　　the pipes.
No, I'm lying! The Old Man did come down the mess-room
Ruddy-faced and full of whisky cheer. He shouted 'Merry
　　Christmas,
Peace on Earth!' We told him to fuck off. Ship's out of beer
(And fags are rare as smiles) but would the bastard let *us* buy
　　Scotch?
Not on your Nellie . . . the cattle might stampede . . .

Later now; I've just come off the bridge. The air's brilliant up
　　there.
The cold's like a telescope. All the coast of Finland is ablaze
And stalactites of light hang in the sky like frozen fire.
Felt pretty low this afternoon, thinking on you at home with
　　Danny and all that.
And me here like I was doing time. Now though (am I getting
　　sloppy?)
In this cheerless, leaking cabin, which could well be a stable,
Maybe I'm learning something about Christmas.

Fri. 23rd

Common lawns getting high. Hope I'm not expected to be gardener
as well.

1925. Half shot; nuns been plying me with sherry.

Polaroids in the kitchen. Betty director of photography. Takes one of Reverend Mother, Sisters G and D, Father Michael and me. All decapitated.

' . . . it's de box, mister.'

Adjust it for her. Next one worse.

Sister G takes one of Betty. Looks like a charred Stalin at the Last Judgement . . .

Wholesome freshness of nuns. Stuns me yet I can't dress it in words. Spontaneous gaiety constant and effortless – like pressure release from a deep reservoir of joy.

Pete parking over the way . . .

Sat. 24th

It's all cat and mouse round here trying to avoid the old dears . . . Mrs Grey lurking among the arbours . . .

Got to queer bar after doing the rounds last night. Yoop there with his phoney friend. Said he'd come hoping to see me. Pretty made-up really; he's a nice fella that Yoop. Pete liked him too. They treated us royal. Slipped me a fiver to get a round in. Didn't want to take it but he made me and wouldn't accept the change. Who's complaining?

Taking me to club tonight. Winchell's. Hope he doesn't bring that fucking Eugene.

Fella parked in mini outside the queer bar – ghastly burnt face like molten cheese. Staring. Eerie.

Letter from A in Singapore. He says: 'I've only got fifty-seven days to do at time of writing so I couldn't give a fuck about anything these days. I'm a bit better off now you've thinned out. I think everybody is, so the bars must have lost a lot along the line.' Y's court case is held up again because Chinese witnesses never appeared 'so you don't need to be told how he feels towards our black brothers'. That's double his time Y's done out there now and he hates the East. I'd swap places in a moment. T has another dose, predictably, and B sends kisses and a smell of his Brut after-shave . . . thirty-two dollars-worth. 'Lads say thanks for the pint' – I sent a note to get a round in . . .

Can't understand why the letter makes me so sad. Mind wings back there and I feel sort of homesick. Think when I'm old and past it I'll look back on those times there as among the best of my life. Most things hereabouts are phoney:

> . . . An' I'm learnin' 'ere in London wot the ten year soldier tells:
> 'If you've heard the East a-callin' you won't never heed naught else.'
> Ship me somewhere East of Suez, where the best is like the worst,
> Where there ain't no ten commandments, an' a man can raise a thirst . . .

If it wasn't for Pete and Agnes I'd say to hell with everything and ship out on a Scandinavian job.

Lunch-time.

Colin and Dansk drew the four to eight watch and took the wheel hour about going down the fjord. To Colin it was like coming home to be lulled by the sway once more and to feel rather than hear the deep incessant throb of the engines. He couldn't explain it but after a few days there was something unnatural about being ashore. You got involved with people and things. You sold your freedom. Oh you could get drunk all right and bang off till you were numb, tell yourself you were having a smashing time, even believe it, but high up on the bridge again with the spokes of the wheel in your hand and the land falling away either side and the bows splaying brine knifing through the water towards an horizon as elusive as a rainbow's end, then the peace descends and you pity the men who live in the houses banked on the hills of the harbour, anchored to monotony . . .

Told Reverend Mother that Pete stays here sometimes and she was concerned. Just now Sister D and the French one arrive with spare mattress, sheets, blankets, pillows, etc. They accepted a drink. 'Whisky or beer?' I asked.

'Whisky of course. Only novices drink beer.' Sister D repeated this in French to the other one who shrieked and rattled off a mixture of French and English all of which was unintelligible.

They laughed a lot and have left a sweetness in the room behind them . . .

Left their drinks too, barely sipped them.

Wasting this weather sitting indoors.

Sun. 25th

Fresh Chapter

In which our hero wins favour with a Patrician and how his wherewithal is considerably amplified.

Shanghaied into prostitution. Thirty quid richer (£30).

Eugene breezes into the office without knocking or anything and behind him is a tall elderly fella, dignified, handsome, immaculately attired and quite stunningly – the word occurred to me as soon as I saw him – Patrician.

Yoop shakes hands and I'm introduced. He looks at me in a way which says he likes what he sees then sits down and accepts a drink.

Whisky flows and he chats genially, asking questions as if his health and happiness depend on my reply.

He's an Argentine. When I say I'm a seaman he wants to know if I've been to Buenos Aires and when I say yes he carries on about the city and gives me his card to look him up next time I'm there.

Yoop rolls a cigarette which we share. A few puffs waft me into a smiling Utopia. The Patrician has a facility for injecting humour into the commonplace. He smokes with an air of naughty gentility and passes it on like one might dispose of a dead rat. My eyes keep returning to him in case I should miss something.

High, but came back into orbit once I'd eaten.

Yoop and Eugene leave immediately after dinner saying they have to drive to the airport . . . and *still* I don't catch on.

The Patrician and me (I) do a pub crawl around Shepherd's Market and finish up in his suite in Gallaby's. I'm pretty drunk but OK really, more buoyed up by the luxury and the attentions of the Patrician than anything else.

We're sitting there drinking and talking and he suggests I 'take a shower before the drink catches up on me'.

Thick fucker! I tell myself. This'd be obvious to a blind donkey and here's you thinking you're swaying the aristocracy with charm and intelligence.

Half expect him to slink into the shower room but he doesn't, just opens the door a crack and passes in a silk dressing gown which reaches to the thighs and feels dead sexy where it rubs the skin.

All he wants to do is go down on me which he does like it's his birthday, grovelling down there (ecstatic about my tattoo) and whelping with his hands frantic up and down my body inside the silk but I don't mind, I just sit there deep in the chair with legs stretched and eyes closed sipping champagne . . .

When he's finished I make out like it was pretty good and he's chuffed because he starts calling me 'dear boy' and 'beautiful boy' and crying and whatnot . . .

Before I leave he slips half a dozen notes into my pocket which I pretend not to notice but count a hundred times in the cab coming back.

Wants to see me again tomorrow. I'm to ring in the morning.

Feel there's the kernel of a story here for Yoop . . .

1130. Modelling this afternoon. Phoney Eugene rings. Photographer friend, etc. 'Uh huh!' says I. 'You caught me like that last night.' He deftly side-steps the abuse I'd prepared and swears it's above board. Five quid an hour. Wanted to send a car, big deal. Said I'd taxi and charge him . . .

Can't settle to *Manicomio*.

Can't settle to anything.

(Bloody Sundays!)

To boozer for lunch-time session . . .

1900. Modelling sexy gear in Pimlico. Quite a bit of fun . . . pleasant food for the ego too. The photographer a professional to his manicured finger-tips. His professionalism contagious. Can't wait to see the pictures.

Mon. 26th

Pete: 'Firty nicker! Where's 'e 'ang out fen, fis geezer? Bit o' powder on the old bollocks an' I'm right in.'

Hero: 'There's more to it than him just turning up and saying thirty quid and here's your supper. It's all psychological; tact's needed. The old boy wants to re-live his youth in a fella and all that.'

Pete: 'I can be suttle – shit! no one suttler'n me when I gets goin'. Suttlest geezer round the 'Stow. I'd make out I wuz floggin' eggs . . .

'Knock knock. " 'Ere cock, fancy some wevos fen? 'En fresh, straight up." (I'd 'ave me foot inside the door by fis time, lookin' sexy, givin' 'im the eye.) "Laid fis mornin' fey wuz, direct from the ol' fowl – no messin'." (I'd be near the bunk by fis time see, 'oldin' up an egg, flexin' the biceps, givin' 'im a bit o' the ol' one two.) "Put you down for a ton fen shall I? You can get your 'ole in all night along the Viente Cinco for a 'undred wevos, wot!

' "Not 'alf 'ot in 'ere is it? 'Ow about a quick shower?" ' '

Folk group Sundays, upstairs in the Welbeck. Crowded. Eager young blades. Birds with long waveless hair, leather minis and necks strung with medallions. Pete chatting up Fat Legs. I get a round in and leave her out. Sensitive creature: 'Don't I get a

vodka?' 'No.' 'Why not?' Tell her I've bought her four already
and unless she gives a written affidavit that she'll come across with
the nooky she can buy her bloody own. Hate birds who flirt and
ponce all night then go home laughing at a fella. Fat Legs a prize
gold-digger; written all over her face. (Pete too fucking cunt-crazy
to notice.) Calls me a bum. Call her a brass nail. Volley of obscenities (the like of which I haven't heard since SD nicked the bike of a
Sikh pissing in a monsoon ditch along the Bukit Timah Road).
Spits at me and stalks out. Bird nearby says 'She's been looking for
that for a long time, the bitch'.

Couple of nurses. Meal in Indian restaurant. Horror Face at his
post outside the queer bar. Want to point him out to Pete but can't
in front of the birds. Nurses home for midnight. Invaded Agnes
and drank her booze. Thence oblivion.

Pete's *giving* me his spare radio.

2100. Lunched with Patrician in Spanish restaurant off Regent
Street. He slipped me a tenner gratis, didn't even go to the hotel
with him . . .

He flies to Vienna tonight but returns in a few weeks. Talks
veiledly about taking me back to the Argentine – no chance!

During the meal he'd lean over the table, even when he had my
full attention, tap my arm with his long delicate fingers and say
'Keiron, dear boy, are you with me?' He pronounces my name
with the accent on the last syllable so in Spanish it must mean 'why
rum?' Guess the waiters thought I was some sort of plonky . . .

2200. Agnes says 'What's wrong with me Keiron? I should be
having affairs with executives and politicians like everybody else . . .
why must it be young men . . . ?'

Tues. 27th

More prancing about on Pimlico rooftops this afternoon. Photographer says he's searched for me for years . . . 'Stallion strength

aflame with aesthetic awareness' . . . (I'm quoting – honestly.)
Could have kissed him. Can't do shorts or bathing-costumes
because of snake – and I'm not showing the world the length of
it . . . not for five quid an hour anyway . . .

Wed. 28th

Party in suite at Gallaby's. Two airline hostesses. Fellas mostly
bent. That Eugene showing me off like he owns me or something.
Everyone pissed.

Yoop tells them about tattoo and everyone wants to see it. Cage
for a while, feigning modesty. Am eventually stripped down to
skiddies. (Can't claim to have offered much resistance though.)

Fella says he wants to lick it all the way up from the rattle on my
foot. Tell him no one's stopping him. He does so, or at least starts
to. He's only reached the ankle when one of the birds (she'd been
in the limelight before Hero arrived) whacked *me* across the face
with her bag.

Party rather broke up after that . . .

Drank right through though . . . still sipping now . . .

2200. Heavy head. Haven't ventured out all evening.

Re-read Bergotte. He fired me with enthusiasm and I settled
down to *Manicomio*; but the fire soon spluttered and died. Kept
writing though.

Feel it's taking on flesh and personality. Flows easiest when
Dansk's not on stage. Can't get him to come on naturally. Could
force him but that'd be me, not Dansky. I like Colin. I don't have
to make him do anything. He has a mind of his own and refuses to
move when I handle him wrong. Anna-Greta's the same. I like
her pouting whorishness and uncanny honesty. I've no idea where
she comes from. Penny perhaps? Anna-Greta's an intelligent slut.
Probably a bit of Penny and a bit of Agnes . . . and a bit of someone
I haven't met yet thrown in.

*

By the time Dansk arrived to relieve Colin on look-out the ship was heaving like a fat drunk in a troubled sleep. Already Colin was soaked to the skin from the spray of the breakers and his eyes stung. By rights the Mate should have called him into the bridge housing in weather like that but, he thought, the brass had it in for him because of the stowaway.

What the hell! They couldn't prove anything. They couldn't even single him out as the one who was goosing her because just about all hands had had a go ... the bitch was public transport ...

Colin shouted 'Force seven and rising'. He pointed toward the Mate hunched under the lamp at the chart-desk. 'Make eyes at how's-your-father and he just *might* let you on the bridge in the event of a hurricane.'

The weather had scattered the words before Dansk could hear them but he understood their import and grinned. Colin exaggerated a shiver and turned to go. Suddenly Dansk was shouting in his ear 'Your girl, Anna-Greta, is in the cabin ...'

Colin called 'She's not my bloody girl ...' but it was no use; he was hoarse already and anyway he was talking into the wind.

He doubled down the companionways, slanting automatically against the roll of the vessel.

The poxy slag ...

The whore ...

She'll get the lot of us in nick ...

From the engineer's deck he leapt over the railing onto the after hatch which rose to a steep incline as the bows nosed into the water. A quick drop and he was running downhill.

I'll knuckle her ... by God I will ...

The seas swelled above him, huge menacing giants, whipped to anger by the wind.

Unwillingly he cowered beneath them. They threatened his own anger.

As he reached the door of the accommodation pocket a wave pummelled the ship broadside and thundered over the main deck all but sweeping his legs from under him.

In the bathroom Colin removed his wet things and showered. Courage returned under the warm water and he determined to take a hard line with Anna-Greta. He wouldn't speak. He'd take hold of her and throw her bodily into the alleyway. He'd lock the door. She could do what she bloody well liked, but not at his expense . . .

She was a fucking nuisance.

Anna-Greta lay on the bottom bunk smoking. She wore Dansk's dressing-gown, the black Japanese one with the dragon embroidered on the back that Dansk was so ashamed of but felt he had to keep because it had been a gift. Her breasts were exposed and a naked leg was raised to the bulkhead to give pressure against the movement of the ship.

She said 'Hi!'

Colin held the door back and jerked his thumb in the direction of the alleyway. 'Out!' he hissed through his teeth.

'Can't someone stop this bastard rolling . . .'

'OUT!'

'Whatsdamatta!' He hated her most when she put on that phoney Yanky drawl. 'Can't the big sailor take a bit of weather . . . ? Gets him frightened does it . . . ?'

'Out you . . . you whore . . .'

'Oh! I'm with ya. You suppose I've been havin' it away with your Dansk . . . your precious cherry boy . . . I doubt if he's got a pair of balls . . . maybe you could tell me . . . huh?'

Colin swooped swiftly and grabbed her wrist, wrenching her towards the deck. She kneed him in the crotch. He bent double and groaned.

She guided him, almost tenderly, onto the bunk where he lay with his hands cupped between his legs trying to lash out at her . . . trying like a dumb cunt to swear . . .

'Oh, shit Col, I'm sorry . . . I didn't mean . . . shit . . .'

She was stretching across him, sucking at his neck, twining her tongue through the terraces of his ear.

'Colin,' she whispered. 'Colin, love me a little. I know I'm a tramp. I've always been like that. There's a devil inside me, kicking, and I must have a man to stop going mad. Funny isn't it? Colin, are you listening to me? It sounds silly Colin but I'm in love with you. I didn't think girls like me fell in love. I've had tribes of men and I've never given one of them a thought beyond his technique in bed. Now, suddenly, this. Everything's upside down.' (Was she really crying?) 'Help me Colin. Help me through the worst of it. It won't take long darling. I've heard sometimes it only lasts a few days. Like a cold. I'll leave as soon as I can bear to . . .'

And it goes on, echoing my mind at the moment:

(Sex. Always sex. Stuffed – up to the neck with it. Sex in the morning when you wake piss-proud; sex all day, creeping into your thoughts like the persistent salesman; sex at night when the lights are down and a look, a touch, a gesture boils in the blood and must out. Loveless sex, shackled to flesh, wringing the heart dry, sowing seeds of disgust, self-contempt, guilt, hatred . . .

Yet ever the need for the body and the warm bed, the need to sink into oblivion, to lose identity in exquisite sensations, the thrill of the final thrust when every nerve stampedes into a riot that for a moment touches eternity.)

Feel now as if I could write all night, though drily, without interest . . .

0100. Insomnia. If I hadn't guzzled all the scotch this morning I might have been able to stun myself to sleep. Now even the pubs are shut. And it's so quiet. Occasional groups of people pass on the street beneath the windows. I hear their voices and the click-clack of their heels on the pavement as they approach and cross my screen, swinging in an arc from street-lamp to street-lamp, their shadows cavorting about their feet like frisky kittens, now to the rear of them, circling rapidly, moving ahead – and other shadows, lighter, longer shadows following the shadows in an endless spectral dance, a dance of shadows.

And the clatter and the laughter grow fainter as they pass off my screen and the strangers continue into a void lit by lamps I can't see, streets I don't live on.

I'm becoming morbid, morbid and facetious. Fear. It's closing in on me . . .

I'd go to Agnes but I've been there all afternoon.

Agnes . . . she's becoming a responsibility – not altogether unwelcome, but there's something frightening about a woman in love. She never leaves the flat unless I'm with her; says she's content to be waiting, etc . . .

It (the flat) seems to be in semi-darkness night and day. She moves among the furniture with a liquid grace, like an angel fish among coral. She breathes softly but audibly and is always smiling. A sense of pine and purple pervades the rooms . . .

Afternoons are best, when the kids are at the nursery. We lie in the cool of her bedroom with the light chopped into bars by the slats of the blind. We don't speak much. She clings to me but is not possessive. She's afraid of her age but demands nothing of me . . .

Must keep writing.

So often during the day a triviality dances before my eyes or perhaps an observation makes a lightning flash across my mind rending for a moment someone's everyday cloak, disclosing secrets, and I tell myself: that stone could be a gem; it should be stored in the notebook to be fetched out sometime and cut and polished . . . But always I forget and there's no time and all I set down here are my own drab movements . . .

Father Michael in the rose-garden reading. He nods, curtly. On the cover of the book a representation of the Biscuit. Overpowering; I believe it (I think) but it is overpowering. Immense. It petrifies and compels me. I mean if Christ really is God and the Biscuit really is Christ then . . .

0115. No sleep. I try and try but I'm frightened . . .

Eddie Coulson clinging to me when we reached the ladder. Eddie laughing his little laugh like that. Half of Eddie not there when the wave receded. It haunts me . . .

Words can't communicate . . .

Words are fools . . . words bitter and their lees poisonous . . .

I'm for communicating in flowers and perfumes, in rich ageing things, cured rinds and wines and tubs of oil and tallow, brasses crusted with verdigris, rotting timbers in old barns, the music of sudden wind-gusts in summer, shells like miniature cathedrals and strange and shapeless sea things like footprints in the clouds.

Words stale crumbs in my mouth tonight. I've got the 'nausea'. Fear of the dark and the quiet. A stifling claustrophobia in the universe. Locked in an oven . . . trapped in a mine . . .

Alone! Utterly!

Perverse and insignificant!

Urgent need to expiate. Evil to be lashed out of me; scoured out of me. Desperation and a demanding God. Words no use. Words felons. Words demons to take me over the brink. Something. Anything but think. Shake this off . . .

Thurs. 29th

The world is bathed in gold today and all five senses tingle with the expectation of something new and glorious. The sun has tamed the wild cats from the building-site who come slinking up the High Street where shopkeepers (who are only known to smile on the first real day of summer) fling scraps to them and housewives without coats and pimply delivery boys smile at them indulgently. Even the tramps feel festive. The locals' sense of brotherhood hasn't extended to them yet but they've developed a warmth among themselves. Just saw two outside the cake shop sharing edibles from a paper bag, passing it politely from one to the other like Quakers.

It's dangerous to walk through the rose-garden . . .

Got drunk on my way to lunch simply breathing in the barbarous perfume of the flowers. Too much for frail mortals. Even now I feel a compulsion to leap down there and stuff my pockets and capture in my hands that gorgeous effusion, to store it all away against the winter and the cold. It seems impossible that you couldn't keep it fresh somewhere if you cared enough

58

. . . then again I feel that about the snow sometimes too . . .

Must be somewhere to swim around here; it's one of the few things I'm any good at, swimming.

Bad for a while last night . . . an anguish I can't explain; the booze catching up I guess, or pressures and nerves and things. Thinking too much about God and that seems to spark it off as well.

As it happens I finished up having a good giggle . . .

Memory confused. Briefly:

Ring the club and they send Jock, the chauffeur, to fetch me. Think he's a bit daft and only knows he's a Jock because that's what Yoop calls him. Place not too full. Eugene and Yoop with fat Philippino who smiles but never speaks and two studs who turn out to be rum fellas – Geoff (pretty hard) and Tony (witty). Royal Horse Guards.

In the toilet Geoff corners me at a hand-basin.

'What's your game then?'

'What's it to you?' Nervous; think he's coming the hard man.

'How long have you known Eugene?'

'Not long.'

'Work for him?'

'Hell no!' Then catch what he's on about. 'I mean yea! On the side sort of – if the price is right.' (Big time.) He grins and winks and I warm to him.

In the bar he orders more whisky. Says to get it down me because I'll need it; there'll be a squeeze with the three of us, he says.

Tony makes like he's wanking behind the Philippino's back.

Imagination seethes with erotic possibilities.

In Gallaby's lobby we march behind the Philippino like body-guards shadowing a maharaja. We fuck around a lot in the suite while he's smiling and undressing us. Then we are flustered off to the bedroom. Tony drilling as if on parade, Geoff swinging a bottle and me wondering what the hell . . .

Moons and coos tucking us in, patting the pillows and humming like a pregnant hornet. Eventually switches off lights and tip-toes out shutting the door with a burglar's delicacy.

'What happens now?'

'Wait till he comes back.'

'How long . . . ?'

' 'Bout twenty minutes.'

'What gives?'

Geoff shrugs. The bottle passes around and we have a good laugh. After a while: 'Who's got a tab?'

'They're with the gear. All I've got's a hard on.' I'm in the middle and simultaneously they each rub a thigh with the nearest hand.

'Fancy a wank then?'

I assume indifference but mumble 'Wouldn't mind I guess'.

With one movement they heave me over onto the deck. 'Go ahead then; we won't say nothing – only fetch the fucking tabs first . . . '

'Lazy bastards!' Wrap a towel around and step back into the other room. Almost fall over the Philippino on all fours with his eye to the keyhole and Jock, hat in hand, shunting away behind . . .

Geoff and Tony are rolling on the bed with laughter.

No siller; Geoff says Eugene will pay us.

In the bar last night he (Eugene) said something about there being a cheque for me in the post – payment for looking after the Patrician. Told him I'd been paid already and immediately wished I'd shut my mouth.

He shrugged, supercilious, 'We pay escorts. Gratuities don't concern us . . . ' Phoney prick!

The day is dying, but splendidly and from my window all London is on fire. It takes me back to those mellow afternoons at the orphanage when I used to lie by the hour in the long grass of the downs and dream wild impossible dreams till the sky blushed and the sun hid its face . . .

Fri. 30th

Pete betraying himself in ways I find endearing.

He has been speaking of marriage as if it's a movie he's going to

60

. . . and then only because the bird wants to see it. I had thought he was frightened. He sort of shuffled when he spoke of it and looked up squinting as though the sun's too bright . . . 'Oi dunno fough; might change me mind . . .'

But last night drinking he spoke for five hours solid and the truth emerged. He *is* frightened but not of marriage itself. He's frightened that something might go wrong with his business, that he mightn't be able to support the bird and kid, that he mightn't be the paterfamilias all the way.

Also he's frightened that his affection for her mightn't last. ¶

He's working harder and making more money at the eggs than I'd thought; has all sorts of schemes for expansion on the drawing-boards of his imagination . . . a new van, bulk shipments from Denmark, investments in poultry farms . . .

Just before we go to sleep he says: 'Forget about i' anyway – I'm talkin' like a bleedin' Yank . . .'

Poor old Horror Face still stationed outside the queer bar as we passed last night. Chills me to see him; as if the temperature has suddenly dropped.

Was in Rio once during the Mardi Gras when a reveller flung a plastic mask onto a bonfire in the Praca Maua. Remember watching intrigued as the flames licked the false face and the heat melted the plastic which softened, sagged and ran into hideous folds, rippling swelling pouches which banked up one on another, burst, and splayed the molten substance onto the crackling pyre.

The grotesqueness of that mask as the flames tongued through the hollow eye sockets and started to melt the plastic was cauterised on my brain and when I see that fella's face it's a sort of recognition.

Gallaby's tonight and I've already shot my load twice today with Agnes . . .

Sat. 31st

At breakfast I said that when I was in Port-au-Prince a few years ago I had narrowly missed seeing Papa Doc. You'd have thought the hounds of hell had been unleashed. Betty went white . . . (I'm not joking) . . . blood visibly drained from her face and she flung pots and saucepans and frothed at the mouth. The anger didn't appear to spring from within herself. It was more like a foreign force, a possession . . .

Generally though relations with her have improved. She has even taken over as my personal dietician. Lately she has been declaring that kidney is brain food and I'm to eat it for 'de book'. Kidney every meal. I masticate and swallow each mouthful reverently like a religious rite half expecting a great fire of genius to break out in my head. If, in future, I go any length of time without kidney I'll feel I'm starving the brain . . .

Strange, this unquestioning credulity, yet isn't it on just such that civilisations have been erected and have thrived?

Got Mrs Grey and a couple of the old hens half sloshed in here at lunch-time. Reverend Mother none too pleased.

Father Michael tells me one of the ones from the main building won a thousand quid at the Camden Town Bingo Hall last night. Had a heart attack on the spot. She's in hospital. Doubtless Mrs Grey'll furnish details when she sobers up . . .

Copies of photographs. Pretty smart. Modelling clobber doesn't half make a difference. Took them over to show Agnes and now she won't give them back.

Sun. 1st

Sundays heavy ashore!

Would like to take a bus heading nowhere, go there and do nothing on arrival.

Those mad nights in Brazil . . .

Mon. 2nd

Had appointment at Gallaby's last night but didn't go. Fuck them!

Father Michael in here till after 0200. He reads sections of *Manicomio* but passes no comment and I find this frustrating.

He questions me about myself, my background, where I've been, what my interests are. Without thinking I find I'm telling him the same lies I tell at Gallaby's . . . pat little fictions to adorn a drab history (though they're as legitimate, I guess, as a woman's make-up . . .).

He shows interest in the sinking of the *Tidepond* so Hero enlarges on it and tells him about Eddie Coulson. He reads *Two Swallows*. When he's finished he grimaces with imagined pain and says 'Ugh! The poor fellow.'

I say 'Bloody lucky if you ask me Father. Think of all the trouble it would save . . . '

'I doubt it. The condition wouldn't negate the desire. If anything it would aggravate the torment . . . '

'Torment . . . ?'

For a second he smiles wisely then switches the subject to Agnes. I tell him she lives in Grove Gardens and that I see her most days. He wants to meet her.

I like being with him. Feel I'm with one of those Greek philosophers who gathered youth around them and played midwife to their unborn ideas . . .

This exquisite day has drifted into an exquisite evening and I'm loath to spoil it. It's one of those rare evenings which will lose its enchantment if you so much as move. In the country you can amble through fields and bathe in the essence of it; in the highlands you can scale the summits and brush your fingers along the sky as the evening flares and crackles all around but cities swallow the magic . . . unless you're very quiet . . .

Tues. 3rd

Albino and an Italian fella. Coining the lolly. If only the bastards didn't want to kiss you . . .

Cheques always signed Peter van Leer. Where the hell is Virginia Water?

Where the hell is Yoop for that matter? Haven't seen him for days. The phoney one has taken command. Today he is a whirl-wind of charm. I've got looks, figure, personality, style. But sartorially I'm a bum. A man should be as presentable in clothes as out of them.

The Company will outfit me . . . no cause to feign indignation . . . the Company proposes to pay . . .

Stunned with alcohol.

Wed. 4th

Geoff said when he was stationed in Germany he had to fly from Frankfurt to Venice to lie in a coffin while some geezer wanked over him!!!

Eugene's suavity. Detest the bastard when I think of him but as soon as he speaks I knuckle under. Was pissed after yesterday's lunch-time session but he persuaded me to collect a client from Heathrow.

No trouble in recognising the loud-mouthed Yank. Told me straight off he was a professional golfer.

Top class, he confessed.

In Kensington he decided to drink in a club he knew so Jock drove on with the luggage. He needed a 'piece of ass' and 'that goddam Gallaby's wouldn't know a piece of ass if it saw one'.

His club was a damp basement floored with linoleum and papered with travel posters. Pieces of ass not in evidence. He sprouted money and announced that he was after a piece of ass.

Sympathetic sycophants fell over one another to produce a little tart, hewn from the brittlest flint, who miladied her advantage and drank highballs which she pronounced like a piece of ass should (what are highballs anyway?) and all the while I was 'buddy boy' and 'pal'.

Admit to stimulating civilities to some uncouth Australians, a thing foreign to my sense of fitness, until I could take no more and told him I was leaving.

Dashed back here for boiler (incidentally Horror Face was parked opposite my window, staring; had to draw the curtains) then to Knightsbridge pub to meet the lads. Geoff and Tony were there all right but so were Eugene and the bloody golfer and a half a dozen other people, two of them horrendous queens.

As soon as Pete arrived I passed the word and the four of us retreated singly by different doors and made a dash for it in Pete's motor . . .

After that a handsome, boozy night.

Came back at all hours and the four of us kipped up here. Geoff and Tony went their way this morning still half-pissed. They've got a parade or something this afternoon. Pete's taken with them and they with him.

1830 hrs. Agnes's.

The soothing balm of her devotion . . . like having another dimension to crawl away to when this one gets over-pressured.

The Hero just arrives nowadays and goes straight to that cool bed. Sometimes she lets me sleep, though more often she spends the time massaging my back and legs with magic fingers . . .

She never demands anything. If I haven't any more energy for sex I simply don't take the initiative. She doesn't question it. Seems most happy when I'm doing what I want . . .

Ironical when a fella's got to creep to a woman's bed for sexual recuperation . . .

Thurs. 5th

Story of Bergotte's in *Esquire*.

His appeal very special, very personal . . . writing an extension of himself . . . projected personality.

Sense of contact difficult to explain.

Some writers make me itch for a pen, some leave me breathless at the end of a book, some lead the way to unexplored territories and point out horizons I never dreamed existed yet Bergotte's the only one I feel I want to meet . . .

Relish the art in Hemingway but I'd run a mile to avoid the man. Jean-Paul Sartre fires me with a zest for thought but I'd rather chat to an old AB or a miner. Wouldn't have minded meeting Genet once, accidentally, when he was younger or Oscar Wilde when he was older . . . fellas like Graham Greene and Solzhenitsyn I think would be too reserved unless you knew them well over a period of time . . . Hopkins I worship; but preferably through his poems . . . No! there's really only Bergotte . . .

I wrote to him a couple of years back though the reply like everything else went down with the *Tidepond*. He gave me his home address and phone number in case I was ever on the California Coast. Meant to reply but kept putting it off and putting it off. Now I guess it's too late . . .

Stoned out of my mind again last night and wild . . .

I'd already been upstairs with one geezer but felt a compulsion to drink and returned to the club. One of the drag queens was miming a number. Eugene said 'I'll give you ten pound if you'll show your tattoo on stage.'

'Pig's bum, cheapskate. Twenty.'

He didn't flinch, just handed me four fivers with his sour milk smirk.

Peeled to briefs in the dressing-room and wheeled on stage behind the drag queen. Gyrated around and made out like I was goosing her. She was singing that song 'It Could Have Been Any Guy' and couldn't understand why everyone was laughing . . .

Only stayed there half a minute but it went down well. Everyone howled 'More, more' and the queen thought they meant her. Geoff and Tony kept slapping me on the back after . . .

Caught no sight of him but know Horror Face was there. Can *feel* when he's around.

He haunts me, though gently . . .

Told Pete about screwing the albino and the Italian the other night. He mocks 'Cor . . . fuckin' Jack-a-randy!' Asked him where he got the word but he couldn't say. We rolled it around on our tongues. Eventually this profound ditty was born:

> Jackarandy, Jabberwocky
> Very handy, very cocky
> Very cocky, very handy
> Jabberwocky, Jackarandy

Fri. 6th

Back from Agnes's. Little Mark walked into the bedroom while we were on the job. Agnes very upset. Can't see why myself. The kid seemed singularly unconcerned . . .

Sat. 7th

Promised myself I wouldn't speak of *Manicomio* here but I spend a lot of time on it and my mind is geared to it. The other night while some geezer was sucking me off I tied a knot in my hair to remember that Dansk plays a guitar . . .

The whole conception's wrong. I don't need a reader to tell me there's no hope of publication but I get such satisfaction out of working on it. Hell, in this Babylon where flesh and lucre preside with a power the Kremlin never knew a fella needs an airing-room.

To write simple things simply . . .

Halted by painting of St Sebastian in the National Gallery. The body shimmers with those illusive qualities which hold me captive . . . sensuality and spirituality . . . can see it vividly in my mind now but must return to study it more closely.

Feeling I know the person . . .

Dansk?

Sitting here in fine raiment . . . feel empty, purposeless . . .

Measured amid a debris of threads and cuttings in a Jewish tailor's under Frith Street. Eugene assured me the old hawk is one of the best in London . . . inconceivable that Eugene'd patronise anyone else.

Aquascutum, Harrods and a wild shopping spree with me as the incidental model. Not once consulted (wisely I guess) so evinced a determined lack of interest which wasn't too difficult because I was still with St Sebastian and Dansk and beside them Eugene's flamboyance was grotesque and unreal.

In the motor he took proprietorship of me announcing plans for a rosy future. Sickening. Had a mad desire to laugh into his face and dash off and ship out to Madagascar or somewhere, leaving him a little pool of loneliness surrounded by his miserable acquisitions . . . a traveller stranded when the last train has pulled out . . . but he's as insensitive as a rubber ball and'll keep bouncing into eternity . . .

oooo hrs. Back from Gallaby's. Exhausted. A Canadian kid. Fucking beautiful. And so genuine. Why does a fella like that feel he has to pay for it?

In the mirror – my youth passing like landscape from a railway carriage . . .

In the heart – longing for love, a boundless longing for God . . . or anyone. Warped by self and mediocrity . . .

In the sky – stars, as splendid, small and isolated as people . . . we try to make contact but our voice is feeble, it fades in the void. Occasionally faint stirrings from somewhere in the galaxy, an attempt at communication and we leap about tuning equipment, searching for a frequency which will deliver us from this loneliness, liberate us from this isolation . . . but always it's a hoax, always an illusion and we should have learned by now . . .

In the night – nostalgia and a murmuring sweetness . . .

In the silence – peace descends like dew . . .

Wish I'd stayed the night with the Canadian kid now. He wanted me to (they all do) but I make a point of leaving as soon as the job's finished. Professional armour, if you know what I mean . . .

Mass this morning. Sat a long while, not praying, just looking, thinking and drinking in the peace.

Wish I was a disembodied spirit; Catholicism mighty attractive . . .

Off to Welbeck for dinner-time session.

Am supposed to model this afternoon but will go to Agnes instead. I need her these days . . . she's a lifeline . . .

Mon. 9th

Reverend Mother rings. Stranded in Golders Green. The convent car spluttered and died and she's pushed it into a side street. Do I know of anybody . . . ?

I take a cab. She stands on a corner by a lamp-post and I can't resist saying 'You look like a streetwalker, Reverend Mother'. She throws her head back and her laugh bounces among the buildings. 'At my age?' she gurgles.

The motor parked at a crazy angle off the curb. Taxi-driver gets the bonnet open and fishes around inside. Don't know what he does but it only takes thirty seconds.

Drive back with nuns. Two sisters in the rear, young attractive French girls bubbling with high spirits. They joke and clap and flirt all the way to the convent. Reverend Mother tells me not to encourage them or they'll be losing their vocations.

Agnes's birthday yesterday. Had forgotten. Rang Father Michael and took them both for a meal in a quaint restaurant near the Post Office Tower. A wine called Bull's Blood. He wore civvies and she was rigged out in soft patterned things. They hit it off well together.

A genteel but tipsy old woman at an adjacent table whispered to me 'Your parents are absolute darlings – so happy!'

Wonder if Father Michael guessed I'm knocking her off . . .

Tues. 10th

Toothache all morning but better work in spite, or perhaps because of it. Dansk has a seizure on stations and is logged for being drunk.

Took Penny to lunch in a St Martin's Lane pub. Good spread. One of her bosses there with his secretary. Penny ordering 'another slice of ham and a cognac' while Whiskers and his oh-so-smart sup halves of bitter. Penny sure can see her booze off. She got kittenish walking back to work and we kissed in the middle of pigeons, seed-throwers, Horatio – everyone. Was in half a mind to whisk her off to a hotel . . .

Tony in Knightsbridge with a dead sexy looking fella called Tom. I asked what nationality he was. He said 'Part Irish, part French, part Italian, part Slav . . . '

Tony: 'Really! How sporting of your mother . . . '

The three of us got bevvied and moved on to a club in Belgravia. Smart place, small but intimate. Woman who owns it sits on a high stool, all bust and arse in a black dress with ten tiers of pearls and a picture hat heavy with flowers. A dog the shape of a rolling-pin knots its leash around the stalks of her stool and is disentangled ritually every fifteen minutes. Clientele mostly army or ex-army. Older men look like Evelyn Waugh; their wives have long slender legs and are agreeable. Younger fellas look ripe for promotion.

Picture Hat is a social Brigadier. Privilege is paid for with brandy and Babycham.

She takes a dislike to me in general and my ear-ring in particular. Soon she asks scornfully 'What sort of man wears an ear-ring anyway?' and rolling-pin yelps from the cave beneath her chair.

I say I'm Romany. I mean it to be a joke. I've been saying it for years. (What else can one say?)

Interest flares. Much whispering. Seems everyone has a soft spot for gypsies. I can't go wrong. I don't say much more but booze pours in from the Evelyn Waughs and their agreeable wives and the lads beavering for promotion.

After a while even Picture Hat gets in on the act and I'm made a member of her club.

Half sloshed when I came back for the boiler. Turned in for a couple of hours. Rang Eugene and the limousine (can't bring myself to call it a car, 'Rolls' sounds a bit pompous and 'motor' under-rates it; it's a cross between a taxi and a hearse) will collect me around ten. Apparently Jock will recognise the Zambian at the airport.

Can't remember ever having had it off with a coloured geezer . . .

Have worked it out that at the present rate of income plus interest I'll be in the six figure bracket in less than a hundred years . . . making no allowance for expenditure and loss of earning potential, that is . . .

Wed. 11th

Nothing much. Tired and bored.

Dull and humid outside. Intermittent drizzle as if the heavens are past weeping for humanity's sins . . .

Even *Manicomio*'s become a tasteless, flaccid task. Wrote the simple logging scene over and over before lunch and tore it all up straight after. Frankly I'm sick of being chewed off. Three times last night in as many hours. Apart from the Zambian – who, incidentally, was white and a big schoolboy to boot – I didn't even know their names.

. . . And that fat Yank's wife stuffing herself with chocolates and gurgling into the phone and him not bothering to close the bedroom door. I'll tell you, that bar in Gallaby's, for all its British reserve, is nothing more than a meat mart.

Fitting for suits this afternoon.

Thurs. 12th

The old tailor told me about the Oasis this afternoon and sent his boy to show me the way. An unlikely building at the end of Shaftesbury Avenue. Too many in the pool for any real swimming but a tonic to plunge in and mess about. Spoke to no one yet felt a part of the place just being in the water.

Rode back slumming it on the top deck of a number thirteen. Walked through the Park to avoid the Indian restaurant Pete and me (I) did a moonlight from last night. We slipped out wraithlike and ran up the High Street, vaulted a hedge and lay low in someone's garden listening to the racing feet and angry voices of the waiters. Pete prided himself on his astuteness and maintained, though with little conviction, that the 'fuckin' coolies is bleedin' the fuckin' country and the sooner fey take the 'int . . . '

Had we been caught it would have been me 'wot 'ad no principles, leadin' God-fearin' zitterzens orf the straight an' narra . . . '

Later in the room, hunched over cans of Newcastle Brown, I read a couple of pages of *Manicomio*. It confirmed my worst fears. 'Fuckin' shite . . . '

A writer's mortal sin is to underestimate his reader.

His cardinal sin is to overestimate himself.

Radio Czechoslovakia on Pete's transistor. A woman called Judith (or is it Ruth?) speaks at length and vividly about a church in Prague. Iron-curtain countries talk of nothing but themselves. Even their constant cool is hysteroid.

Father Michael rang. He says 'I am alone and wish to be entertained'. Could have suggested Gallaby's but he would not be amused. He's coming over at 2000. Hope he doesn't want to go on the piss. I was looking forward to a night off.

0300 hrs. We've been drinking sherry and talking. Time doesn't exist when you're talking to him . . .

But you don't really talk to him; rather, he tells you what you want to say in words you'd never have found yourself then answers himself with a few brief, static phrases which seem to pinpoint the problem perfectly. Then he gives you credit for the whole thing, looking at you as though he esteems your intelligence.

... Get the feeling he should be a mystic but clings to the clay; that he's being purged in a river and is swimming against the current. He seems to live in the dark yet the light shines from him ...

Could grow to worship him in a way – but he wouldn't allow it ...

(Wonder what he'd be doing if he hadn't become a priest.)

Fri. 13th

Friday 13th. Great day for the superstitious. Nothing this end though. Life has fallen into a fairly regular pattern – *Manicomio* mornings, Agnes afternoons and whoring at night. Pleasant enough but I was better off at sea dreaming about such living ...

Sat. 14th

Drove with Agnes and kids to Richmond and picnicked among the trees. Might just as well have crossed to Regent's Park. Wish she wouldn't get so affectionate in public.

She lives in a dream world ...

Sun. 15th

Hectic night at the club. Drunk on spirits and abusive. Geoff and Tony had to bring me home ...

1900 hrs. Afternoon modelling in a Clapham studio. Two snooty birds who wouldn't speak. (Believe I bring out the worst in women.) Blonde one had to lie with her head on my crotch. Went to the piss-house and had a wank beforehand but still got a hard on.

These shots should be good though if the tattoo shows up right . . .
Playboy-type stuff.

Mon. 16th

Suits at last. Don't half look smart.
Can't wait for Pete to see them . . . I'll be cool as hell . . .
Full day.

Tues. 17th

Much I want to put down here but can't marshal my thoughts. The
more that happens the less time I have to record it . . .

Horror Face in his mini everywhere I go staring at me like a
sphinx . . . gives me the willies but I feel sorry for the poor
cunt . . .

Wed. 18th

Am getting nothing written.

Sick to death of sex. And my nudger's sore too, strained with
overwork.

A Froggie with a nasty chin tried to get stuck up me last night.
He's licking my arse out and before I know it he's near half way
home. I've never fancied that and if ever I do it'll be for more than
that bugger can afford. Swung him a hell of a crack in the jaw with
my elbow anyway, and he took the hint.

Thurs. 19th

Off swimming.

The days grew longer and warmer after the foggy turbulence of the Channel but the vast ploughed field of the Atlantic, huge rolling barrels, haled inexorably into the sun.

Time was suspended for Dansk during his watches on the bridge. It was his oratory, his solitude, his private sequestered gazebo. He did his thinking there, faced fear and elation. Dreams were born there and he dreamed them through.

Dansk loved the sea; he loved the sea as it was then when bank on bank of high impregnable rollers marched like advancing giants across the ocean, each picking the ship up like a toy, holding it to the light for a moment then dropping it casually in a hollow to be lifted by those behind and all beneath a dome of serene blue, fringed with a soft white down.

(There is no argument with the sea, no quarrel. To imagine so is absurd. It is her suzerainty and she is the mistress; we are ever the strangers, the pilgrims, the tiny caravan trudging the wilderness. Sometimes, as now, we encounter her armies on the march, no telling where they come from, no hint of their destination. We ask questions among ourselves, grow apprehensive and prepare paltry defences. But they never attack. They might play with us as soldiers play with the stray discovered in the camp, throwing it from one to another and laughing at its needless fear, but this is only the boisterous excess of their spirits, never evil, never malicious. And if we are bruised we have no legitimate complaint for *we* are the strangers, *we* are the foreigners. She opens her country and gives us the freedom of her highways but she stamps no passports, issues no guarantees of protection.

At other times we are caught in the thick of her battles, dazed with terror and panic-stricken in the face of a violence beyond our understanding; no place to hide. But we cannot claim that she is attacking *us*, that we are any more than accidental witnesses to her wars.

People speak of the 'angry sea' and the 'cruel sea' but they do not know her. She is neither angry nor cruel, treacherous nor aloof. She is a woman. *The* woman. The archetype eternal woman. If a man must know her he has to live with her, in her, on her, not waving goodbye to this shore or counting the days till that, not complaining too much of her violent whims or rejoicing too much in her calm. He must learn to know her as a man his mistress, as a subject his queen, as a pupil his teacher. She has hidden treasures to delight, sacrifices to ask and commands to be obeyed. She has an infinity of secrets to disclose but too few real lovers . . .)

What was that star I set myself the other week? To say simple things simply . . . ?

Fri. 20th

Lunch-time. Eugene and Yoop bring Sunday's photos to the queer bar. Smashing – even if I say so myself.

There is one of that blonde piece and me (I) walking away from the world. I think we're hitching meteors. It says a lot about youth and love and looking for God.

Amazing what can be done in a Clapham studio . . .

They want me to do a series for *Ganymede*.

Yoop vacant-eyed and jibbering with nerves. Drugs I reckon.

Sat. 21st

Tons of world news but don't want to refer to it . . . tons last year too . . .

Betty's homespun homilies. Feel she's gradually accepting me. Yesterday: 'Dem de Lord chooses to curse he gives a fine face. You get yourself a plain girl Keiron mister.' Can't think what brought that on.

1930. Agnes asked me 'Did you ever sleep with Eddie?'

Said 'Of course' (wildly untrue) just to hurt her. Why the need to hurt her? Her love and submission bring out a brutality in me . . . at times I want to crush her . . .

If only she'd stand up to me now and then – at least it would give me an excuse to cut her down.

Sun. 22nd

Flogged a geezer with a studded belt last night. Said he needed to see the sheets soaked with blood. Don't think I did it too well but I've no experience.

Only a young geezer, early thirties, tough looking too . . . I'd never have thought he was the sort to grovel like that . . . and with such single-minded intensity.

Fucked him in the finish and had to gag his mouth to stop him screaming for it. Later in the bar he says 'I don't want you to think I'm queer. I'm happily married with three sweet kids. It's just that sometimes . . .'

Mon. 23rd

Fella in Gallaby's wanted me to fly to Amman simply to post a letter. Offered £50 with the return ticket.

Tues. 24th

Much activity but monotonously the same. Even Winchell's cheques arrive with dreary regularity.

Manicomio a wash-out. I'll never make a writer.

Wed. 25th

I'm alone on another planet. Cold dry deserty landscape. Stark mountains in background. Suddenly on the edge of a jungle (or it might be a cliff) the nuns are mixing mortar by hand and moulding blocks. They have laid the foundations of a building. They greet me civilly but without interest. I am hurt. They continue working.

I ask if I can help. Reverend Mother points to the mortar. I work, then they are all gone. I can't see them but I know they're not far away. Perhaps they're praying. I sweat over the mortar, anxious to finish the whole building before they return. I want to please them. I want to be accepted.

I ask Reverend Mother what they eat on the planet. She points to a tailless round-rumped cat in a tree. 'Ibox' she says.

I swell with admiration for them. They arrive with no fuss and set about building. They are dedicated to God and hold no store by human values.

A treacherous wind blows down from the mountains and swirls up the dust on the plain.

The nuns are gone again and there's only me and the stunted ibox and the wind.

I'm frightened. The ibox starts to laugh.

I look at it. It's Horror Face.

... If you don't set it down within seconds it's gone like a déjà vu ...

Thurs. 26th

Pete came round yesterday evening. He needed a hundred quid. Something about an egg shipment from Denmark. He explained the scheme in detail but I can't make head nor tail of things like that. Said I'd take the money from the bank but found I had enough in cash. Gave it to him. He was embarrassed though I can't think why. Apart from the satisfaction of giving (for a change) I consider it a kind of duty of friendship and loyalty and that. If our positions were reversed I'd think so too.

Anyhow it's cheap money.

Apart from that I think he's a bit disgusted with my carry on.

We went to Knightsbridge and Geoff talked him into coming to the club. He's always backed out before. We were hardly in the place before a fella was chatting him. The fella was pretty blatant but it didn't matter, Pete took it as a giggle and threw him some choice repartee but apparently in the piss-house he made to touch Pete up.

Pete was wild about it when he came back to the table. He didn't even sit down, just told me what had happened and left the club.

Geoff said 'What's up with your mate?' so I told him. He said 'What's he a virgin or something? I thought you two were shacking up . . . '

That grated me, especially coming from Geoff.

Hell, I can't picture Pete as a bed-fellow . . . I mean, what would we do . . . ? (apart from laugh . . . ?). It just doesn't figure.

I don't reckon Pete'd go with another geezer. It's not on his menu . . .

Fri. 27th

Mrs Grey highly excited. Her family congregating here Monday for a reunion. Her ninetieth birthday. She stops me in the rose-garden and tells me about it for the umpteenth time. 'You must come and meet everyone,' she says. 'I'll be particularly pleased you see because the young ones will think I'm just an old fogey – but when they see I have a young friend . . . Monday afternoon.'

I said OK and walked off but she hobbled after me – awkwardly, like an albatross coming in on land – calling 'You won't forget, will you? Promise you won't forget . . . ' She looked so absurd and so simple that water gushed to my eyes and the old emotions went haywire. I had to get away quickly. It's embarrassing when that happens. A fella feels soft and stupid. She probably thought I was damn rude.

Off swimming!

Sat. 28th

Father Michael came to the boiler house. Said he'd been given tickets for the theatre tonight and would I like, etc. Had to say no because I'm meeting the Patrician at the airport.

He said 'You appear to have a lot of friends arriving at airports'.

I laughed. 'Darling of the jet set,' I said. He didn't laugh though. He looked at me curiously and for a moment I believe he could see right through me.

His eyes weren't accusing but they said '*Whore*'.

Trying to work on *Manicomio* but have no inclination for it. It starts off all right but weakens. Dansk won't live. I push him too hard.

Meeting AG the actor this afternoon though not for Winchell's. He's a contact of Tony and Geoff. Apparently they were telling him about me and he said he 'goes potty over seamen with earrings'.

2345. Half-pissed again. What the hell!

Felt an idiot tonight. Jock drove me to Heathrow. Was groomed and preened and polished to meet the Patrician. Did my job; arranged luggage, tipped porters, fended off newsmen (there weren't any), was charming all the way to Gallaby's and the dago bastard was as impersonal as a frog. He was dragging an Austrian kid with him (good-looking, I'll give him that) no more than seventeen but thick as they come and smouldering with avarice.

There was an accident on the Chiswick fly-over immediately ahead of us. A Volkswagen rammed a Zephyr and a truck joined in somehow, I wasn't watching. We were held up for half an hour and heaven knows what queue formed behind us.

Worst was the blood spurting from the face of the woman who ran screaming into our headlights as Jock jerked on the brakes.

And the Patrician looked stonily ahead . . .

And the little Hun sniggered . . .

I'm getting out of this rat race . . .

Sun. 29th

I don't understand anything. Life's got out of hand. I always thought I could step aside and look at myself dispassionately, as a third person, but everything's gone askew lately. Everything has . . .

Guess it's the attention I've been receiving. Apart from the warmth of Agnes there's consideration and very real affection here at the Convent, and abroad, in the dark cul-de-sacs of the night, a novel importance and, in lust, the shimmying possibility of excitement . . .

(I'm pissed tonight, Journal. Everything's fucked. It's not that I'm depressed. Wish I was. In a way I'm happy as hell.)

Almost nothing written for days. Rarely find myself here and when I do I'm tired or drunk or just plain bored. I'd like to make a resolution, set a deadline day or a financial target then chuck this whoring in – but, shit, I'm incapable of keeping resolutions . . .

. . . Not that I always shack up with these fellas. Half of them simply want company as far as I can make out. I take no notice of what they say any more, the introductory advertisements, the surface waves. They haven't learned basic honesty. The honesty of Gide. The honesty of Genet. Honesty with themselves. Their eyes are full of loneliness and emptiness and fear. It's as if they've sold their souls and haven't been paid . . .

I approach them blindly now. After half an hour I can predict what role I'm expected to play and I'm almost never wrong. I look at them as characters in, say, a Graham Greene story, characters who have a message to convey but are unaware of it in their banality.

The new wardrobe's made a difference – the tweed suit especially. (Can't bring myself to say *my* wardrobe; it hangs over my head like What's' name's sword.) Can go anywhere now and don't feel too out of place. Eugene keeps telling me to take the ear-ring out but fuck him. I've worn it since I was fifteen and I'm not removing it now for nobody. It's the one thing that reminds me I'm a bum seaman . . . that's about all I've got left to be proud of . . .

That Eugene's only a pimp anyhow. He hates my guts. After last week's photos he suggested I might do some pornies. (You know, I reckon he fancies my body on the side; you want to see the way he stares at me sometimes when he thinks I'm not looking.) Normally I wouldn't give a damn, especially seeing Tom was there at the time and I guess the idea was that we do them together, but

I felt (again) that he was trying to manipulate me, like a puppet, so I answered with an emphatic NO. Worst of it was the urbane bugger didn't bat an eye. In fact he made me feel he was doing me a favour and I was stupid enough to turn it down. I could feel him smirking . . .

He stands for everything I hate in a man.

Every time he rings about a job he hints photographs. I meet his clients but get a great kick out of vetoing his pornies . . .

. . . There's more to things than meets the eye . . . can't even begin to explain so I'm fucked if I can figure it out . . . I'm no James Bond . . .

Must turn in now. The whisky's finished and my mind's a field of storms . . .

The bunk's empty and looks uninviting . . .

Could go to the club . . .

Or to Agnes's . . .

Wish I had someone of my own . . .

Mon. 30th

Swimming all morning . . .

NW8 swarming with Chinese each one speaking a different language . . .

Will pop down and move among them then escape to Agnes's . . .

Tues. 31st

Up-tight. *Definitely* finished with Winchell's. Rang the phoney and told him so.

Couldn't read or write or anything. Wandered in the rose-garden. Wasn't sulking or angry . . . too many thoughts conflicting in my mind. In no condition to analyse them . . .

I just want *out* . . .

Looked for Father Michael but he was away.

In the boozer Yoop said nothing but I felt he understood me. He's weak, that's his trouble . . . and I've got an idea he's pretty fond of me. I reckon if I got him alone and said 'Come on, you and me'll shoot off together and forget this circus' he wouldn't hesitate. Eugene's got him under his thumb . . . and I guess the dope's got a lot to do with it . . .

Don't know why but I'm important to that Eugene. I'm not as professional as Geoff and Tony or as good-looking as Tom but he needs me. He was pleading, even threatening in the boozer though I can't figure out why. There's a jigsaw here but I don't have all the pieces. What's more I don't want them . . .

I just want *out* . . .

They can have their gear back if they force the issue. I want to forget I ever got tangled up with them.

. . . And that cunt suggesting I'm out to blackmail. Hell, I wouldn't know how to go about it. What do you do? Ring Scotland Yard and tell them prostitution is rife in Gallaby's? That Winchell's supply studs for rich poufters under the guise of an escort service?

Might as well tell them pigeons are shitting on St Paul's . . .

Or maybe I write to the wife of Joseph P. Schmudt or whatever the cunt with the camera was called and tell her her old man's a pederast and I can provide photographs for a consideration . . . She'd probably send a wad of dollars to add to her album and they'd ball each other perving on them . . .

I'm not capable of blackmail.

Promised to go to the party Saturday but that's final. That's it.

Not long before I'm ready to ship out anyway . . .

Oh, and another thing. Horror Face was in the bar sitting right alongside us. He must have heard every word we said. I didn't know it was him. I was only conscious someone was there keeping very still and quiet, well muffled. When I saw his empty mini outside then I knew . . .

He wasn't there by coincidence either. Have never seen him in the bar before and anyway he's never around lunchtimes . . .

And another thing. It's him that's written those letters. I know that. Don't know how I know but I know.

*

Can report that the daughter from Hong Kong is alive and well and a hard-faced self-centred looking bitch she is too.

Wed. 1st

Sheer sensuality of waking up. Sunlight streams dustily through the windows picking up objects and laughing at them. It adds a new dimension and colour to my mermaid who basks in its rays and winks when I move.

A new sort of life is beginning, a life lived in sunlight with visible daytime people. Leave the dark to the bats and the cats and the lizards who live under the rocks . . .

Pete sleeps quietly. He's late for his eggs but I'm loath to wake him.

. . . At home again . . . I've a pen in my hand . . .

Pub in NW8 last night with a bunch of students. Delightful pimply one called Cary. After an hour talking he asked me 'And where do you teach?'

Pete said ' 'm teach! Be fair. 'e couldn't teach a bloody sparra. 'e's a seaman.'

A four-eyed squib said 'You're very articulate for a seaman'. Felt like planting him. The arrogance! The ignorance!

I'll tell you, you'll find more sense among fellas who ship out than you will among the would-be students sitting around trying to sound intellectual – whatever the hell that is . . .

A mind is no better for having been beaten into shape by the schools. Formal education is well enough for the umimaginative who must conform but it never produced Shakespeare or Genet or Conrad or O'Neill – or Christ for that matter . . .

Half-licked cub!

1730. With Agnes most of the day. She's bugging me a bit. When I go to the flat she's whimpering all over me and when I stay away she's a long-suffering martyr . . .

She keeps referring to the *other woman*. Haven't the heart to tell her it's an army of other men so I say it's Penny.

She hangs her head with fatal resignation ... Blanche du Bois playing the biblical Susanna ...

If she's in love with me OK, I'm flattered, but I've made it pretty clear that I'm not in love with her ...

What the hell does she want from me? I screw her don't I? And I never charge ...

I'd bum her out except that she's become a habit ...

Thurs. 2nd

All morning helping to install a new deep-freeze in the kitchen. Had to dismantle the door-frame and the reconstruction job isn't one of my most artistic achievements, but the door closes. Once we had it secure in the niche nuns and old dears stopped by to admire while Betty said a sort of Mass on it clacking and clucking and turning every so often to bestow a benediction on the congregation.

Lunched in the parlour with Father Michael. We spoke of sex and physical beauty. I said 'You contradict yourself – it's sinful to yield, impossible to ignore and repression hatches a score of evils. What the hell's a geezer supposed to do?'

He quoted Hopkins:

'... How meet beauty? Merely meet it; own,
Home at heart, heaven's sweet gift; then leave, let that alone.
Yea, wish that though, wish all, God's better beauty, grace.'

I said 'Great! Next time a naked virgin lures me to the couch I'll repeat that. And a fat lot of good it'll do me ...'

He still thinks I'm a Catholic. Wonder if his interest in me would change if I told him I wasn't. As far as I know I'm not even baptised.

(Don't like to say this, him being a priest and all, but I reckon he fancies me ... or have I got a hang-up these days thinking everyone fancies me ... ? Trouble is most do ...)

Swam all afternoon at the Oasis and fell asleep on the sun-deck. Surprisingly few there considering the glorious weather. Perhaps all the regulars thought it'd be overcrowded.

A little girl with insane eyes followed me everywhere staring at my navel. Several times she stuck a finger in it. Eventually her mother carted her off with pathetic apologies.

I didn't mind a bit – honestly . . .

Fri. 3rd

THE KETCHUP KID

When puffer fish, that tasteless dish,
Assume their ilk's disguise
They inspirate and so inflate
To twice their normal size
And human kind's not far behind
When human kind's ambitious
To emulate, like a certain Mate,
The absurdities of fishes . . .

Such classic mien had not been seen
Since the days of pomp and splendour
Though that noble mask made ratings ask
Pert questions re his gender.
Well it once befell that this likely swell
On stepping aboard from shore
(He'd had a few but it wouldn't do
To suggest that he'd had more)
Stretched out for a while in languid style
Beneath an after awning
Where cadaverous Walt, a mischievous salt,
Descried him in the morning.
Now this officer lay with his feet of clay
All twisted on the deck
And the look of the dead on his epicene head
And the thickness of his neck
Prompted our man to conceive a plan
Which called for a knife clutched tight
Besmeared of course with tomato sauce

Running freely left and right.
Then he issued screams which shattered the dreams
Of the braided, bearded Master
Who clomped to the spot at a dignified trot,
But when he beheld the disaster
He too let out a terrified shout
And summoned to his aid
The quack (the sod); the Arm of God;
Police, priest and Fire Brigade.
In a second or two the entire crew
Had gathered on the scene
(The men hid their faces in case there were traces
Of smiles in between)
And the officers said 'The Chief Mate's dead',
As they turned from grey to yellow,
'And by his own hand, we understand,
Tut tut! Such a competent fellow . . . '
Then chaps from emergency gathered with urgency,
Flocking around by the score,
And declared with conviction that not even in fiction
Had the dead been so dead before;
Till amid this tableau of mourning and woe,
And grief and lament and all that,
Our protagonist stirred like a newly fledged bird
And the Captain smelt a rat.
'Oh he's definitely dead,' the Doctor said.
'The diagnosis needs no question . . . '
Though subsequent snorts from the wretched corpse
Smacked rather of indigestion . . .

Well the earth was moved and enquiries proved
That cadaverous Walt was the sinner
And was transferred for his crime to the Shaw Savill Line
Where he quickly grew thinner and thinner.
But our Saucy Blade was covered in braid
And revered as a living martyr
And was given his ticket, which is only cricket,
And an OBE and a Garter.

So the moral is this: Let Fate take the piss,
For her blessings are blows in disguise;
Just sit back and let her, she does it much better
Than anything we can devise.

1600. With Pete for a lunch-time session in a Dalston boozer
when in walks MT, same crooked grin, same cocky gait. Was made
up to see him but discovered in no time that something was
missing. He tried hard but the old M was finished, dead. A year
married and he's full of 'responsibilities' and 'plans'. 'You don't
know what you're missing Keiron,' he kept saying. 'A fella hasn't
lived until he's married.'

I nodded away saying 'Great, Mickey, great' but he knew I
didn't mean it. He knew all right and felt himself superior locked
away in his little world . . .

Hell, when I remember those times we used to have as kids . . .
the night on the Blue Flue job we dived overboard and swam
ashore in Hong Kong harbour when the Old Man refused to put a
liberty boat on . . . the time on the *Remuera* when we gatecrashed
the passengers' fancy-dress and won the prize for originality . . .
the time we smuggled a taxi-load of birds past the cops in the
Royal Docks by getting them to flash greasers' ID cards and say
they were queens in drag . . . hell, the dozens of times recklessly
drunk in honky-tonk ports and not giving a damn . . .

His missus came in after a while and she was quite a darling.
Maybe M was trying to act up to her image of him or something.

They invited us back to their stable but we got out of that.

Worst is, Pete'll go the same way . . .

Fuck it! All this depresses me.

AG, the actor, rang but told him I was staying in. Nice fella and
good conversationalist. Would have gone over if I wasn't expected
to screw him.

Finished up taking Penny out last night. A drink in Gallaby's to show them I had a bird but there was no one there except the Patrician and his male impersonator, then to Knightsbridge where we met Tom. Penny fell in love with him but he was off to the airport so she insisted on coming back here. She had always loved nuns, had often thought of becoming one herself blah blah blah and anyway she had her period . . .

Rang Father Michael who met us at the door of the main building. On the stairs the incredibly old nun who's a bit dotty meets us holding a paraffin lamp. She speaks in French to Father Michael who reprimands her. She cowers and retreats, swinging the lantern above her head. At the turn of the stairs she wheels round and spits out obscenities. Father Michael answers in expressionless monosyllables. She falls to her knees and blesses herself.

Penny looks on all this with a compassion I never thought she had.

In his rooms Father Michael explains how the old nun's father was a parish priest who had lived with a woman (this in the last century) and raised a family of five before his bosses found out. He committed suicide by impaling himself on the tine of a brass crucifix. It obsesses her in dotage.

We got stuck into a bottle of sherry and Father Michael went to work on Penny. In the space of an hour, without using a word you wouldn't hear outside the East Ham High Street, he had exposed the lonely, frightened, affectionate girl beneath the accumulation of defences. (She was still an idiot, but a sensitive one.) She was charmed to death. He could have had the drawers off her she was so made up with him . . .

It was pretty spectacular. He's a perfect psychologist.

Later she was getting sloshed so we put her in a cab. Sat around talking till after three. Again he brings the subject round to sex. I think he wants me to commit myself to some personal details. I ask why he harps on it. He says 'You seem to forget I read parts of your *Manicomio*'.

'Does it show a preoccupation . . . ?'
'Certainly.'
I say 'You want to read my Journal'.
He replies, with mock horror, 'I do not'.

A glorious day, lazy, sultry and a mist (it isn't a mist really, more
of a haze) makes the convent and High Street appear to be floating
in a nebulous nether world. A scent drifts in through the open
windows too. It reminds me of something way back, something in
the classroom or playground, something that slips away like a fish
from the hand . . .

Bloody party tonight. The Phoney One has already phoned,
soft-mouthing. They're picking me up in the limousine to make
sure I go. Tried to talk Pete into coming with me but he's got a
date with the affianced and anyway 'No self-respectin' eggman'd be
seen dead at one o' y'r cake an' arses . . . '

Sun. 5th

Stoned but alert. An alcoholic second wind.

The last of the Yorkies has flaked so I'll get this down while it's
fresh.

Drove towards the South Coast. House white and colonnaded,
floodlit from the grounds. I thought of *Brideshead*.

Bald-headed geezer opened the door. All arms and kisses
declaring he hadn't seen Eugene for aeons, what a thrill, and who
was his splendid friend (me)? Music noise and people in the room
he led us to. Introduced to many as Eugene's splendid friend.

Affable Yank from Chicago who knew the boozers round the
Federal Marine Docks. Swore he'd met me there. Another affable
fellow with hair lip. Group of young airmen in uniform being
swamped by geezer who looked like Oscar Wilde. Airmen's faces
fresh and simple and wholesome. Believe they thought they were
in society.

Three Yorkie lads as out of place as onions in a fruit bowl.
Wanted to talk to them but was cornered by a fat German.

Eventually rescued. Moved from group to group. Drank beer from a magic pewter pot which never emptied.

Steamed up with the booze and mellow. Baldy laid a hand on my shoulder. The other boys were at the pool, why wasn't I with them? Said I was easy and he led me off touching everyone he passed on the arm. Oscar Wilde was swamping the Yorkies who looked bewildered until Baldy scythed them up. 'Don't monopolise the boys, they're off for a dip.' And in a louder voice to the room 'Everyone's at the pool'.

The pool no Hollywood affair but inviting under floodlights with weeping willows dipping their fingers in the water on the farther side. The guardsmen and a few other fellas already splashing around. Number of older men in suits and ties standing about a kiosk like an ice cream barrow drinking. Baldy said 'You boys change in the shed. You'll find costumes on the pegs.' (Grateful for the trunks because I thought maybe we were expected to swim nude. I'm not too well hung unless I've got a hard on – then I'm as good as many and better than most. Can never figure out where it all goes.)

Got on great with the Yorkies. They're only kids but they're no fools. They were sharper than the airmen.

They'd been invited straight from a Soho boozer. 'Nowt like this round Leeds,' the little one kept saying. He'll be glad there isn't when he wakes up. He's got a shiner on his right eye, spewed on the way back in the limousine and at the moment is sprawled on Pete's bunk and so white you'd think he was dead if he didn't snore so. The long-haired one is foetuled in the armchair. The other, Jim, who is trying to grow a moustache, lies naked on the bed. (No orgies; their clothes are drying.)

Anyway . . . I don't know how long we were in the pool. Do know I was sloshed. Remember clinging to the side bar while champagne was poured into my mouth. All pretty decadent but none the less enjoyable for that. One or two of the men watching jumped in or were pushed in. Lot of squealing and shouting. Everyone became boisterous and tore at the airmen's trunks. Then everyone tore at each other's. I (patriarch) wandered off mumbling 'Kids' stuff'. In the shed a Guernsey fella who would have looked better with his clothes on sat drinking whisky from a bottle. He said that if the bastards thought he was arse they'd best think again ...

Drank with him then threw up outside the door. Stretched along a bench.

Woke and the lights were off in the shed but the door was open a crack near my face. The floodlights showed that the pool was bubbling with rain and drops beat loud on the roofing too. The men were gone from the kiosk and my trunks were drawn down around my knees and I had a hell of a hard on and someone knelt in the shadows alongside me stroking it. Couldn't see any more than an outline but watched as he fondled away.

My head was splitting so that to move would be like having a saw going through it. It was cold as well but I didn't let on I was awake. Then his mouth went to work and I felt the old surge of wanton pleasure ... the mastery in lust ... the mighty, arrogant contempt for everything that isn't self ...

When I'd shot my load he slunk away.

Dressed and carried my head back to the house through the rain. Still quite a few there (the airmen dashing about in underwear like virgins at a dockers' picnic) fairly drunk mostly and desperate. Couldn't figure out who the phantom gobbler was. Baldy said the others had left but they'd sent the car back for me. It was ready when I was but surely there was no hurry. Gnawed at a leg of chicken. Put away a couple of beers. Hung around absorbing blandishments. Slipped out to the front of the house.

The limousine was parked half way around the island out of the glare of the lamps but I could see Jock with his chauffeur's cap at the wheel. Ran round the driveway through the rain and jumped in the back. Had the pewter pint in my hand and was filling it from a bottle of Bass. Finished pouring the Bass, tapped on the dividing glass with the empty bottle then, as the engine revved, I leaned out the window to fling it into a flower-bed and there, standing on the lawn like a statue was Horror Face.

The old eerie goose-pimply feeling got me. I shrunk into the seat as the limousine sped down the drive and turned into the open road. There was no traffic apart from the odd transport lorry and as our lights flashed off white-washed posts and the trunks and branches of wayside trees I seemed to see Horror Face lurking in the darkness between them.

Some way on the lights picked out a tableau of bedraggled, soaking figures in Leeds United scarves half-heartedly jerking their thumbs. Jock pulled up, not too willingly, and two of them got in dragging the other who had been battered about.

Seems some fella touched him up around the pool and he threw a wobbler, taking wild swings at everybody. Took half a dozen of them to hold him down. They'd been in the rain for hours, they said, trying to hitch a lift. Looked for the time and my bloody watch was missing. Took it off in the shed and must have forgotten it. No sweat; will charge it to Winchell's.

Have done the boiler so think I'll get turned in. Trouble is my mind is awake and active, always racing ahead of itself. But if I don't kip now I'll be shattered later.

My eyes keep returning to the kid Jim on my bunk. His buttocks are perfectly rounded like a globe of the world and covered with a barely visible white fuzz which splays out from a feather of hair in the small of his back. His legs are solid as stanchions and the soles of his feet are tough and calloused and a brownish-yellow tobacco colour.

The innocence and trust of him awake a protective instinct in me . . .

Sunday afternoon. Placid day.

Woken lunch time by Father Michael who came to borrow Orwell's essays.

The battered kid who was bathing his eye opened the door. Thank God it wasn't the Reverend Mother because, though we were partly covered by the sheet, Jim's head was nestled into my chest and his arm encircled me. Father Michael said nothing though . . . his eyes betrayed no criticism . . .

Eric with the long hair made coffee while I showered and the battered one, with an ingenuity no artist could capture, told him, without undue detail, what transpired last night.

The kids took to him and he to them.

He's like a physician who has diagnosed a patient and pre-

93

scribed a cure while still exchanging preliminary pleasantries. Don't know how he does it. Don't even know if he knows he's doing it. His technique is different from the one he used with Penny. She needed a bully, they needed a hero. All things to all men. Yet always with a disciplined modesty.

(They never knew he was a priest; wouldn't believe me when I told them later.)

He left and we made it to the Welbeck. At closing time they took the tube to King's Cross. They're apprentices so can't make much. Slipped them a fiver for a drink on the train . . . the rush of joyful bafflement to their faces . . .

It burns to think of them, though sweetly. Jim wanted to give me his address but I said not to bother. Why flirt with impossibilities?

Told him I'd see him in heaven.

Yoop rang. I asked about Horror Face. He was evasive and suggested he might be a friend of Eugene's. Rang Eugene who denied knowing him. When I persisted he claimed it was unethical (if you please) to disclose professional confidences. Asked who was screwing whom and felt him seethe. Yet he galloped on like a thoroughbred. He had an *assignment* for me. I was the only one who would do . . . it would mean a great deal to all of us . . .

Hung up. Then removed the phone from the cradle.

Mon. 6th

Strange letter in the post, half humorous, half obscene. Unsigned. Probably Pete, trying to be funny.

In the rose-garden just now Father Michael turns on me. 'What do you mean by bringing those boys to the Convent?'

I think he is feigning indignation. 'Picked them up in the 'Dilly. Thought the influence'd be salutary . . .'

He is serious. He spits out 'Understand that this is not a doss-house'.

He pauses then adds in a lower tone 'Arrange to indulge your vices elsewhere . . . or *get out*'.

I say 'What's that supposed to mean?' But he strides off – or tries to. I rage. I jerk him back by the collar. Feel like smashing him full in the face . . . but know I won't. Can barely open my lips. 'Just explain what that's supposed to mean . . .'

His dignity is terrible. He stares at me but says nothing. His personal power frightens me and increases my rage. Abuse in my mouth but I clamp my teeth. Release my grip on his collar and return here shaking.

Mrs Grey in the room. She's going potty. Starts flapping her arms wildly, like an excited bird. 'I've a surprise for you, I've a surprise for you . . .' and carrying on about her Chinese ancestors . . .

How much am I expected to cope with in one day?

Must keep cool. Cool is essential.

Will cross to the Welbeck now for a beer and then to the Oasis.

Trouble is my eyes are watering . . .

Fuck him . . . !

. . . Some people go down to Sodom on a return ticket – a rainy Sunday perhaps or when the night's long and they can't sleep – but him, he lives there! Oh he mightn't venture on to the streets and mix with the people, wear their clothes or speak their language, he's too much of a coward for that; he ekes his life out peeking from behind the vestry curtains like some spinster aunt . . .

1645. At the pool an American fella called Rufus. In UK to avoid the draft. Honest, brooding eyes which pinion one then wander off. Also a fine body which seems new to him, as if he's just assumed the tenancy of it.

. . . Wonder if I'll be turfed out of the Convent now. Hardly matters. I'll be off the sick list and shipping out soon. It's just that I thought I might take leave from the General Service Contract. *Manicomio* and all that. Anyway I like it here . . .

Why the hell did Father Michael show such an about-face? Do

you think he might have been testing me? It was a pretty blunt way of doing it. He might be chuckling to himself now thinking he's affording me some sort of crisis – well he is! I'd ring and have the whole thing out except that I'm not sure of his motives.

I mean, what else could I have done with the kids? Left them on the roadside in the middle of nowhere? Has he never heard of the Good Samaritan? Where are you supposed to look for Christianity if not in the Religious Houses? If the salt of the earth . . . oh bollocks!

Trouble is, he probably thinks I *was* having it away with Jim. Well why doesn't he come straight out and ask me? Hell, I wouldn't abuse Reverend Mother's hospitality by bringing anyone back here for sex . . . the narrow-mindedness and complacency of avowed Catholics . . . priests anchored in celibacy ride the tides in the harbour and imagine the rest of us ashore, errant in the fleshpots . . .

Nothing's as simple as that.

I'll tell you, waking up with the kid clinging like that was one of the greatest things that's happened to me. Sex doesn't live in that house; it'd only enter as a burglar, as a thief . . .

I've just thought. Whatsay he's got a kink or something . . . whatsay it's him who wrote that letter? That would explain everything.

Midnight. Told Agnes about Father Michael's carry on this morning. She said 'You put him on too high a pedestal darling, leave him some faults. Can't you see he's a little jealous? Religious people are often like that . . . they're human too you know . . .'

I said 'Jealous of who – the kids or me?'

She smiled and kissed me on the nose. 'Of me . . .'

'Of you . . . ?'

'Mmhmm! He as much as told me so. At lunch-time. He's an extraordinarily honest man. Well darling, don't frown so.'

'At lunch-time?'

'Why not? He's been popping in a lot lately. We have intense talks – mostly about a certain Keiron Dorrity. We've formed a sort of fan club . . .'

Tues. 7th

Reverend Mother rings. Mrs Grey has had a heart attack. She recovers in fits and calls my name.

When I get there the ambulance men are carrying her away on a stretcher. She is unconscious. Reverend Mother looks serene and competent. The debilities of the aged are fuel for her faith rather than cause for alarm. She tells me 'For weeks Mrs Grey has spoken of nothing but you . . . ' And I only stayed ten minutes at her birthday party.

Did Reverend Mother notice I'm pissed?

Wed. 8th

Pete and me (I) with Geoff and Tony and Tom to obscure boozers in back streets. Darts and pints of light and bitter. Good and solid and British. No perverts.

Pete picking up a new van over the weekend. He's elaborating on its virtues when a drunk Yank interrupts with 'Say, fella, what's your accent?'

Pete says 'Culch'd' without breaking his sentence.

Had a Chinese (meal that is) in Commercial Road then to the speakeasy in Aldgate where a girl with a pillaged face had lost a necklace.

All five of us back here in the small hours . . . Father Michael would have thrown a wobbler . . .

Tom's eldritch ideas on the sexual habits of nuns. Have heard many hold forth like that. Is it crass ignorance or a field of humour I'm not familiar with? Or does the devil speak with unguarded tongues?

Thurs. 9th

In the ward the nurse says 'So you're Keiron. We've heard about you . . . '

Mrs Grey sits propped up on a pyramid of pillows waving with not much less than customary animation. Her excited voice doesn't disguise the peace which suffuses her with something like light but which she isn't conscious of. Her eyes are like little brown buttons peeping through buttonholes waiting to be fastened. They are not so quick to move but have gained a lustre . . .

When I see her I smile with happiness. It bubbles up in me. I can't help it. I know she's dying and so does she and her joy is infectious. Are the dying always like this . . . or only the aged?

I've never had much contact with death . . . except my own which shadows me quietly . . .

God! The tranquillity of her. The radiance despite the inane things she says. Her face is as wrinkled as a stewed prune and her breasts don't even indent that absurd pink bed-jacket yet her beauty entrances and beckons me. There is an aura of intense spirituality about her, the perfume of angels, and I think of Dansk.

I kiss her forehead and the flowers I've paid a fiver for look worthless weeds. She holds my hand and speaks to me, sometimes in English, sometimes in French and sometimes with a sort of desperation she shortly forgets . . .

I like holding her hand. She has one foot in heaven and at a pinch she can pull me in . . .

Midnight.

Agnes pregnant. Saw red. Whacked my knuckles across her face. Kids cried.

I said 'Is that how you got Eddie to marry you . . . ?'

The hurt in her eyes indescribably sad . . .

I'm a bastard but shit . . . she *must* have done it purposely . . .

Fri. 10th

Fuck Agnes!

Fuck Eugene too!

He rings. I tell him he's arse. Then I feel ridiculous. Ring back to say if he rings again I'll be over with a few others to fill him in.

Then I feel more ridiculous. Can always have the phone disconnected – but I'm away soon so what the hell . . .

Manicomio an absolute balls-up. Sick of it. It lacks density, it lacks style. It lacks verisimilitude.

2300. At the pool the Yank, Rufus, asks 'Where were you yesterday?' Thought he'd missed me until he says *he* was in Lisbon . . .

Am sure he works for the CIA or the Mafia, he's so evasive when I question him. (Unless, of course, he's in underwear or cosmetics or something.)

Nice fella though. Nobody's fool.

Father Michael in kitchen this evening. Didn't refer to the other morning yet I detected a stiffness, a distance. He wasn't relaxed. Neither was I for that matter. Told me the old boy whose place I'm taking here has left an unexpected fortune to the nuns. They're in the red so that's a windfall.

I don't think Agnes has told him anything . . .

The night is a shadowy canvas with a wind on it painted in silver. Outside the streets are wet and reflect two lights for every one and wheels splash up fire as they pass. Earlier, at rush-hour, the homeward traffic inched along at a mourner's pace. It was dry then.

Sat. 11th

Sister T arrived in a flurry at the boiler this morning (I was up at six) saying sssh, she wasn't supposed to be talking before Mass, but could I come quickly. An old dear was in her room howling like a dog and they couldn't force the door. Climbed over the roof and dropped down to the ledge which barely provided a footing. (At four storeys up the Hero was shitting himself but having a dozen womenfolk breathlessly dependent on your prowess pumps the adrenalin wondrously.) Had to kick the pane in. The old dear had barricaded the door with all the furniture in the room and was squatting in a corner. She looked quite pleased to receive a visitor. Later they took her away.

Father Michael can't have said anything to Reverend Mother. She treated me royally.

Driven back from the pool in a grey and gold Aston-Martin. Sensation of speed even doing 20 mph along Baker Street. Pedestrians gaze in admiration, motorists in envy. Rufus couldn't come up for a drink but will Monday . . .

Sun. 12th

No call from Agnes, no note, nothing.

Feel she must be suffering.

I'd go round but I'm too bloody proud.

Betty very good to me nowadays. A wonderful boost to see that fat black face light up when I stumble into her kitchen and to watch her drop whatever she's doing to prepare 'some'in' special tasty'.

Photographer hasn't rung so I guess my modelling days are at an end . . .

Another dreary Sunday . . .

Perhaps I could take a day-trip to Sodom . . .

Wish I knew Rufus's phone number . . .

Tea-time. Plunged in the deep end. Rang Father Michael and invited him over for a drink. He says 'About time!' A few minutes later he strolls through the door and stretches himself leisurely in the armchair.

'Well – apologize!'

I apologise.

'Good. We know where we stand.'

I tell him I don't, that I apologise simply to keep the peace. Say I did nothing to incur wrath, except be a bit hasty in the garden perhaps.

He crosses himself in mock horror and says 'Jesus, Mary and Joseph – you're intractable! Would you rather I ate humble pie in front of you?'

I shrug. 'If you feel you should . . . '

He throws up his arms in a gesture of despair and walks to the windows. I reckon he's smiling. I pour drinks.

I ask if he's seen Agnes lately and he says no, not for a day or two, he's been busy. Then, spinning round suddenly, 'Did she tell you I visit her? She wasn't supposed to. I'll speak to her . . . '

'Why, Father? Were you afraid I'd conclude you were having an affair?'

He laughs, really heartily. You feel you could write a thesis on laughter when he laughs.

'What do I care what you think?'

'Gosh Father, I might be scandalised . . . '

He laughs louder. 'Good, good. I'll make a note of that. *Engineer liaison with Agnes Coulson* . . . achieve the impossible . . . scandalise young Dorrity . . . '

He is showing a boyish, richly friendly side I haven't seen before.

I press it. 'But would you seriously – I mean like if she offered, would you?'

He sees I'm in earnest and his laughter subsides. He takes his drink and sits again. For a long time he twirls the glass, intent on its movement. Then he looks up. 'Keiron, I'm a priest.'

'Yes, but just say you were in love with her – deeply, maturely in love with her. Would you?'

He says very, very slowly 'I am a priest . . . *first* . . . '

There's much more I want to ask . . . I haven't even begun to explore . . .

He leans over and picks up a page from the table. I've checked it since. It's part of the South American sequence I'd weeded out to throw away . . . overwritten, superfluous . . . but at the time I don't know which page it is:

He opened the doors of his imagination wide as he focused the lenses on the scramble of boys fighting and laughing and sliding over the rocks which rose from the sea, wet now and glistening in the morning sun like a pyramid of gold coins swept up from the ocean bed; naked brown bodies, whooping and yelling, splashing the water with dervish energy. Oh the designs of them . . . bronze gods . . . firm young saplings . . .

The eyes of the binoculars transported the bodies almost to within touching distance and the burning in his loins surged up to inflame his mind which wove and cavorted and panted among them like a dream in search of a dreamer.

On the lower slopes of the rocks small breathless boys sit tensed awaiting each successive advance of the sea as it swells round their feet, embraces their buttocks, lifts them high, laughing as the brine tongues kiss and caress their faces, shouting, gasping, grasping at the lace edges of the sea which plays quick fingers down their bodies and flees like a hastily departing seducer, slipping between rocks in a flurry of foam.

Sweat dripped from the doctor's forehead and the breathing from his throat was hot and jerky. One hand feverishly stroked the idiot's head while the other pressed the glasses to his straining eyes as if to force the bathers nearer.

Older boys stand erect, proud in pubescence, on the higher shelves. One, tensing thews, springing on toes, arms stretched straight as planks, leaps, the body a bow, a spear, slicing the air, the flash of a disc at the neck, the taut flesh of a back glistening. Splash! Slivers of sun splinter the water.

'Quicker, quicker!' coaxed the doctor drawing in his paunch and moving his mid-section in rapid spasmodic thrusts as his fingers tore and twisted at the idiot's hair.

Shouts at the big negro youth stepping sideways down the cliff path from the road, arms dangling, head high, smiling, teeth like white fire in the black face. They swarming him shouting, laughing, scrambling up from the sea, wet feet padding wet rock, gangly limbs flicking water, heads shaking hair flicking water like wet dogs, pushing him laughing to the escarpment, seizing ankles and wrists, swinging him, throwing him laughing over the edge, spinning like a dancer, laughing, splashing the length of his long body in a sudden sea spout of gushing silver . . . a quick lily.

'Bastante! Enough!' moaned the doctor dragging feebly at the idiot's collar as a rider stays a wilful horse. 'Here muchacho,' and he tossed the binoculars into Manuel's lap. 'Look through these,' and he pushed him to the end of the seat.

It was always like that.

He reads and slides the paper back on the table. 'Well, continue . . .'

'What was I saying? Oh yea . . . would you, as a priest I mean, go to bed with someone you were *really* attracted to . . . anyone I mean, Agnes, Penny, one of the Yorkies, me . . . ?'

He bursts into laughter again but doesn't answer my question. The laugh is so unforced it embodies a bit of an insult.

After a while he says 'Tell me Keiron, would you consider yourself a homosexual?'

Instinctively, impulsively I say 'No!' then qualify with ' . . . not really. Why ask?'

He doesn't answer. His silence, as always, is disconcerting. His eyes are turned staring fixedly at nothing and he appears to have forgotten his own question.

I blurt out 'What constitutes a homosexual? If it's a single act then yes, sure, I am. If it's a hundred acts, I am – but if it's an attitude of mind then I wouldn't say so . . .

'You can't cubbyhole individuals into sexual types any more than you can cubbyhole them into anything. There are as many shades of sexuality as there are people with the equipment and the emotional need . . .'

He is looking at me, a wry wise smile flirting between his eyes and the corners of his mouth. He is really enjoying himself.

Wanted more than anything to tell him I'm a prospective father.

Mon. 13th

Horror Face is the mystery letter-writer and the phantom gobbler – neither of which comes as much surprise – but he's Winchell's pay-clerk as well. In the post is a cheque with an accompanying note which carries on about the glories of Virginia Water. I discover what should have been apparent from the letters – the signature is the same as the signature on the cheque – Peter van Leer. I'd always thought it was Yoop.

I've finished with all that mess. What does he want anyway – love? I've not much left and I want to save it.

Have been calculating: with this cheque I've made close on a grand since coming here. Never did have much sense of the value of money. Have always splashed it about like water but this stuff more so. I seem to want to squander it, to lavish it on other people, like guilt.

Would make a strong point by sending the cheque back but find an iron fist inside me gripping it tighter than I have strength to wrestle with.

Last night with the lads in Knightsbridge. Pete drove over in his new van – a Ford Transit. 'Not bran' new,' he explains. 'Li'l ol' lady kinda fing . . . low mileage . . . go'-i' for a song.'

The wedding date's not fixed for some obscure reason, but it's soon, and with the larger motor, business will forge ahead. (He's reticent about his new life. These things are on his mind all the time yet I've got to pry them out of him. It's as if he wants me to think of him as an irresponsible greaser still shipping out.)

As if to distract from his budding kulak status he produces a porny book – two birds and two geezers, all in colour, imaginative, erotic.

Tony says 'Didn't know anyone was watching or I'd never've . . . '

And Tom 'It'd be OK if those two cows'd fuck off . . . '

The Guernsey fella in a torn plastic raincoat sitting alone over half of bitter. I nod to him. He sees me and quickly thrusts his hand into his pocket. He is wearing my watch. I walk over and slip it painlessly off his wrist. He doesn't say a word. As we are leaving he comes up and says sorry, he hadn't known it was mine, thought it belonged to one of the queer bastards. Could he buy me a drink?

On the phone Penny says I'm neglecting her so tonight it's her flat. So long since I've had a bang-off I'm beginning to forget what it's like.

If Rufus isn't doing anything he might fancy her flat mate . . .

Tues. 14th

Agnes persists in wandering dolefully through the back streets of my mind. I want to forget her like I want to forget the Winchell's crowd.

If it brings her any joy I'll admit I'm fond of her. More than I thought I was. But she's old enough to be my mother and anyway . . . hell, I don't know. Just want to forget her . . .

Good night last night.

In a Stratford boozer the garrulous landlady says 'I'm not a good person. Never! I don't want you to go away with that idea but last month my friend and I we went to Lourdes. Lovely? You'd never believe. The candles, the crutches, the people . . . I cried all the time . . .

'But I'm not a good person. Heavens no! God forbid . . .'

Took beer up the flat and lolled about watching tele. Did a lot of smooching.

The girls made supper then we paired off and turned in in the only bed.

Rufus so damn nonchalant . . .

Wed. 15th

All day a warm inviting rain. People seemed to want to walk in it. The High Street was full.

There's a lightness in me, in my voice and in my step. It's been there for a couple of days. I defer to everybody and when alone find myself gurgling at I don't know what.

Rufus dominates my thoughts . . .

Thurs. 16th

Chelsea and Fulham with a couple of birds – this time of Rufus's choosing. No luck and less desire. Why can't that jejune illogical sex forget itself for more than two minutes at a time? I was sullen and boorish and the evening was unsuccessful. Nevertheless before he dropped me off Rufus said 'Man, you're fine to be with'. My defences crumbled. Could have kissed him.

Strolled around the West End watching people swirl in a never ending maelstrom. Flickering neons reflect on pleasure-hungry faces. Garish. The cheap coffee-shops and strip-clubs and porny-book joints create a fascinating horror.

I feel a disillusionment and a kinship. These are my people; I am one of them. The bums the pimps the whores the ponces, what are we looking for . . . love? Security? Some distraction to pass the time till it's our turn for the black hole at the centre of the maelstrom . . . ?

Speak to a kid with long hair and a face like an angel. He's a butcher's boy from Camberwell and over a beer in a late night place he says 'Nothin' doin' round 'ere no more mate. Since they showed *Midnight Cowboy* every punk in London's moved in on the game. You wanna do the classy gaffs with that whistle.'

I laugh. I look at my reflection in the mirror behind the bar. Yes (I'm surprised) still the same face . . . but I feel old, older than the old grey river that plods this city and has seen it all and carries the weight of it . . .

I tell the kid. 'Haven't been doing too bad of late.'

'Got a regular?'

'You know, a few rich steamers.'

'Yea! Wish I had.'

'No lolly in butchering?'

'So so. It's the bird see. She's in the club an' . . . well, you know . . . '

'Try the National Health.'

'Yea. I suppose . . . ' He falters and his toughness evaporates.

'If that's your working line mate you'd best get another.'

He's indignant for a while then breaks into a dazzling smile. 'Sorry,' he says lowering his eyes.

Slip him a fiver before leaving and his 'Cor, cheers' is more than I dare expect.

Signalling a taxi beneath the Regent Street arches when Guernsey approaches. Offer him a lift and he mumbles about having no place to go. Brought him back here and he slept on Pete's bunk.

His socks still haunt the room so I've exorcised them with Dettol and opened the windows and the skylight. Touched me for a quid before he left this morning with promises to repay tonight. He has £20 to collect 'off of' a horse but a mate of his who he rang yesterday has the ticket, etc etc ad nauseam . . .

What sort of cretin does he take me for?

At least he didn't steal anything.

The chestnut trees on the park side of the convent appear brave young warriors, stalwart, standing sentry. Today I discover the trunks and Venus arms (little forests of fresh short shoots and green leaves) are stuffed full of cement.

Reverend Mother tells me this house is the oldest in the area and is protected by the historic buildings people . . .

From the window I see dogs shy and spring, sniff and circle each other while people pant and push and bully and bark . . .

Father Michael says he's been to Agnes's flat. He says she's ill in bed.

She'll get over it . . .

Thoughts keep winging back to Rufus. Life featureless till the pool tomorrow.

Fri. 17th

We've barely pulled away from the curb outside the speakeasy when a patrol car looms up and cuts us in. Pete is yanked onto the pavement. An argument, and one of the cops unlids a box. Fred calls 'Is this a bloody police state fen?' They tap the headlamps — 'No lights'.

Pete standing there, surrounded by the four of them, blowing into a bag, looks defenceless and small, a lamb lost and bleating in a storm. I feel close to him. I want to leap out and smash the coppers' smirks into the back of their skulls and take Pete somewhere safe and protect him (which is daft because I can't protect myself). Next thing Pete and the cops and Pete's motor have disappeared and Fred and me (I) are standing on the pavement.

We taxi to the station and are told he'll be an hour or two. We wait in the foyer among shifty-looking characters standing silent and sullen in corners. Plain clothes men haul a brass nail up the steps and her screaming 'I didn't know 'e wuz law, I didn't know 'e wuz law'. At the entrance she hurls herself onto the deck and beats it with her fists blubbering pitifully. One of them grabs her collar and pulls her to her feet. I say 'Leave her alone you big punk', and he charges me fucking and blinding. Fred is superb. He says coolly 'Your muvver, is she? Strong resemblance.' He blusters that we'll both get a fucking kicking as soon as he's finished with her and Fred tells him not to swear in front of his old lady . . .

Somehow all the excitement fizzles out. Later a policeman in uniform who stood through the scene smoothed things over with us.

An hour and a half wait and Fred says there's not much point in me hanging about. I'm going in a different direction anyway.

Guernsey blind drunk on my doorstep. He's still sleeping. Have soaked his socks.

. . . Wish Pete'd ring. Feel wretched for his sake. He'll lose his licence for sure when the case comes up so that's his business buggered . . .

And it was me who talked him into going to the speakeasy too . . .

Sat. 18th

Rufus may ring. He wasn't at the Oasis. I waited all afternoon.

A void in me which even a visit to Mrs Grey didn't help to fill. (She wilts rapidly.)

This infatuation is a burden and I should rid myself of it. I mean, I don't even like him all that much . . .

I do like him, of course, a hell of a lot, but he's tight-fisted and has no personal warmth . . . yet sometimes, through a chink in an unwary moment, I glimpse a flame, which could be a furnace . . . he shuts the door so quickly . . .

I'm not myself. There are two men fighting in me and both are bastards. Hideous, cloying sentimentality. If only he'd ring or come round or I could bump into him somewhere, say by accident.

I'm like an alcoholic who needs a drink to give him the courage to leave it alone . . .

Pete's miserable as well. He tries to laugh it off but I know his castle's crumbled. He wonders if he can ship out again from the Dock Street Pool.

He'd signed the papers for the egg shipment Thursday too.

Everything's a mess . . .

1900. NW8 stands like an Atlantis, still and golden, swamped in oceans of sunlight. But it doesn't help much . . .

Saturday evening and nothing to do. Feel self-destructive. Might as well tag along with Guernsey and see if his fertile mind won't furnish me with some escape. He raises the common lie to a level of consummate art.

At worst I guess I can always screw somebody. There's a plethora of people around wanting to be screwed.

Sun. 12th

Sunday and holy day. To Mass in chapel and dragged Guernsey who fell asleep.

Simple brass bowl of freesias on the altar but banked around the sanctuary terrace upon terrace of roses and carnations and lilies and flowers I've never seen before – yellow trumpets, violet stars, and trails of vivid voluptuous green spilling over floorwards. The perfume of the flowers mingled with the beeswax and the heavy giddying pungence of incense swung from thuribles and I drifted into tranquillity regardless of lousy head.

Was light of step after Rufus rang and in the kitchen Betty asked if I'd been drinking. Jokingly I told her I was in love. Treated to a diatribe on how 'two people carin' for each other is de most wonderful thing on God's earth' which terminated, predictably, with an admonition 'not to go doin' nothin' you might regret before de appointed time . . .'

Is there an appointed time for regret or does Betty have trouble with her grammar?

Guernsey's boozers in Soho and Piccadilly swarm with interest. They are bazaars, supermarkets where the hard sell is ruthless. Loneliness, selfishness and distrust are in the air but no bitterness. Humour is there too and hysterical enthusiasm. Few genuinely smile.

An insignificant-looking fellow spoke to Guernsey in the street. On leaving him Guernsey enthused. Did I know who that was? So and so. Nigh on a millionaire. Luxury yacht. Just back from Florida. Spent hundreds a day. Crazy about flowers. Ten quid's worth each morning from Fortnum & Mason's. Had bought Guernsey an eighty-guinea suit along with shirts ties shoes etc. Also (a practical side of Guernsey's imagination emerges) a suitcase to hold them.

If so and so liked a fella that fella couldn't go wrong, said Guernsey.

Asked if he'd been bunking up with this so and so. He scowled sourly. 'You've got to ha'n't you? It's the same with all these queer bastards.'

Making a synopsis of his divergent and contradictory tales is like summarising *War and Peace* in a sentence but to commercial prospects he's saving up to return to his wife and family in the Channel Islands and to fellow hawkers, millionaires are falling over themselves to provide for him.

His theme at least is consistent and his professionalism unerring.

He appears to owe everybody money.

Agnes taking a back seat in my mind. Have passed Grove Gardens twice today and didn't give her a thought. She's probably better by now. Had she been really bad she would have contacted me.

Women's minds function different . . .

Mon. 20th

Get so drunk sometimes and talk a load of crap, but don't believe Rufus noticed. He's so bloody impassive about everything – except money. Won't spend at all if it can be avoided. At least he's straightforward about it. In his flat (small, smart – whoever he works for maintains it) the drunker we got the oftener he repeated that he'll be worth a million dollars by the time he's thirty. The thought obsesses him though I wouldn't think he's innately avaricious . . . perhaps it's something peculiarly American, as if the house the Founding Fathers cleaned and swept has been taken over by seven devils worse than the first, a border territory where the American Dream is toppling into a hideous nightmare . . .

Still, if I had a million dollars now I'd give them to him, if they'd make him happy.

Would take the full strength of a detective agency to find out what he does for a living.

Tues. 21st

A full splendid day and the sun shining the length of it.

My egoism may be presiding but I reckon Rufus is as chuffed with me as I am with him. He's not fully aware of it because he's had no experience but – and here's the beauty – he doesn't give a fuck. He flirts unselfconsciously, dangerously even. That matter-of-factness is suddenly spiced and ebullient. His cheeks glow. He almost laughs, sometimes.

Or am I interpreting it to my own interest? Maybe he's made some money or something . . .

He drove me down the docks this morning – the hospital, the Union, the Social Security. At the Pool (shipping, not swimming) I arranged extended leave.

Stopped off in the Kent for a quick drink and stayed till closing time. Pints of Guinness and whisky chasers. The place was booming.

Dozens of old faces.

JM can't remember the name of his ship so doesn't bother to go looking for it; bevy of queens off a passenger job bitching P behind the bar who bats back every ball with a genteel stroke; kid from Coventry all embarrassment about a black eye not knowing that, if anything, it enhances his looks – or at least his embarrassment does; a couple I was at sea school with and every word and drink seems worth recording . . . I want pen and paper to hand to give some sort of permanence to every joy but you can't capture the drinking camaraderie . . . almost immediately it comes to the boil and evaporates and hardly a perfume lingers . . .

Rufus didn't say much but I reckon he was chuffed. Drove to the Oasis after the boozer then back to his place where we sat round on rugs talking and watching television. He says I can stay but there's the boiler and anyway I wouldn't trust myself – and he knows it.

Sloppy, OK, but he makes me feel warm that geezer. A music in him touches a nerve in me which soothes while it excites, makes me dream of daft breathless things and think of God . . .

Manicomio a total balls-up and I don't even care; had no idea what I was on about anyway. Maybe if I was to make Dansk an American:

A lad I know has brooding eyes
And storm-black tousled hair,
Yet 'neath the swagger slouch disguise
I see a dawning there.
I see the spume of angels rise
To rinse the stale air.

You have always walked alone
And I the jostled street,
But Fate's sly all-deciding stone
So fell that we should meet.
And I am cut to willing bone
With pain enormous sweet.

Wed. 22nd

Gorgeous morning, one of childhood's.

The sun jumped up like Easter and still dances. Its light, filtering through a mesh of poetry adrift somewhere in the ether, turns the world to gold. (Transient alchemy! Mrs Grey's funeral from Camden Town 1030.) The rose-garden never looked lovelier and the clucking of the old dears makes a hen-run of the Common.

(I'm too young to grow old . . .)

Everybody's bitten by it. The nuns flirt shamelessly and Betty sang all through breakfast.

Won't take the cab. Will leave now and walk across the Park. It would be felonious to waste a drop of this.

1400. Funeral so peaceful I wished it was my own.

Chinese seem to thoroughly enjoy every aspect of death . . . those carnival wakes in Singapore were more Christian in spirit than any burial from a church with a cross.

Walked back with Father Michael. He spoke, very simply, of cosmic awareness . . . our ant-like existence on a small mound . . . the arrogance of each generation supposing itself the apex of civilisation. He says 'Perhaps we are the first Christians, perhaps we are the early Church . . . '

Promised him I'd visit Agnes.

Hardly cremated and already there's an argument about jewels missing from her room. The Hong Kong one's coming the prize cow and accusing all hands. Agatha Christie'd make a best-seller out of this. If there ever *were* any jewels and someone *has* pocketed them I hope it's the Belgian couple. They're human and genial and their kids are civilised.

Off swimming.

Thurs. 23rd

Lousy head from last night but well worth it.

In Soho we meet Geoff and Tony and Tom and make a great night out of it finishing up in a Mayfair club. Eugene's been on to them to talk me into doing porny photographs. Apparently it's Horror Face who wants them. Told them OK last night because I was pissed but this morning am determined more than ever not to – can't Eugene take the hint that I've finished whoring for him?

When they're giving me the chat Tom says 'You can have 'em with a dolly or anything you want.' I say 'If I do them at all Tom it'll be with you', and he comes over all boyish, grinning and eager. 'All right by me,' he keeps saying. 'All right by me.'

Can't tell what Rufus thought of it all. He asked no questions and I offered no information. The lads liked him. Slept at his place.

Oh this hangover ... much debilitated ... will take a shower ...

It's not so much the drink as the lack of sleep. And food.

After the pool yesterday we drove to the 'Stow to see Pete who disliked Rufus on sight so we didn't stay too long.

On the side Pete says to me 'You don't half pick some idiots' and coming back in the motor I ask Rufus what he thinks of Pete and he asks, noncommittally, 'That your buddy?'

At Fred's place his sister's cat is having kittens in the backyard. He's summoned by a burst of ' 'Ere, Fred, the li'l bleeder's droppin' 'em all over the garden'. We arrive in time to see the astonished parent squatting in the throes of parturition and the awkward emergence of her slimy first-born. As soon as it's out she dashes about in frenzied zig-zags, finally hiding herself beneath the shed shaking with fright.

Fred explains 'She's six months old ... start off young round this way ... '

In *Manicomio* I'm writing 'Rufus' for 'Dansk' and he comes across with ease. Strange, they have so little in common ...

Think I'll go over for a lunch-time livener then brave it with Agnes.

2030. Didn't use my key. Knocked on the door. She opened it and looked quite beautiful.

She said 'Hello Keiron'.

Was going to say I'd come for my laundry but it would have been ludicrous with her looking like that. Said nothing.

Stood staring at each other like strangers for a long while then next I know we're hugging like a couple of kids.

Later she said 'I don't expect you to love me Keiron but you can't blame me for wanting a child of yours who will'. And 'It was my idea so the responsibility is mine . . . I would have asked you darling, truly I would have, but I was terrified in case you'd say *no*'.

' . . . And you can be damn sure I would have . . . '

I was lying on the floor with my head in her lap. She stroked my forehead. 'You don't understand me Keiron. You're only a boy. I'm twenty-one years older than you and I'm a woman. I can't expect you to marry me (wouldn't even *if* you wanted to; I made that mistake with Eddie) but I'm human and I must have something. My heart won't take another break.

'Every morning I wake up and think *this is the day*, *today he'll go back to sea*. Tomorrow I'll be some old bird you were nesting to boast about over beer in your mess-halls . . . '

'That's not true Agnes; give me credit for a bit of heart.'

'Oh no darling! I've seen it all before . . . not that it's really mattered . . . ' She smiled, but it was a serious smile. 'But then I've never loved quite so much before . . . except perhaps Eddie . . . yet I think of you both as the same person, almost . . . '

She bent down and kissed me on the mouth. Her eyes were shining as she raised her head. She said 'Keiron, if only you were ugly . . . then no one would look at you, no one else would love you but me.' (I thought of Horror Face and wondered if a lover had rashly whispered that to him one day.)

'Surely you see how much I need this child – it's my last chance Keiron, don't be angry with me . . . ' and so on.

It was always on the edge of my thought to mention Rufus, wondering if she'd understand. Glad I didn't.

The kids treated me distantly. As I left little Mark said 'Don't hit my mother ever again, you!'

Hero reduced to bounder.

Fri. 24th

Lay there admiring bodies.

The sheer splendour of the human form holding a life and beauty of its own, an excellence of quality and colour that transcends mere flesh. Tried to find some reason for the waves of wonder and desire that rose and broke in me looking at the youthfulness of even the most gawky of them and happened to glance at my own torso stretching before my eyes like a log of carved and polished mahogany. I saw it as if for the first time. It was as beautiful as the others and appealed to me in the same way. This came as a shock. I understood suddenly, with the clarity of a vision, that my body is not my own. It is no more mine than theirs is mine, or mine theirs. The pleasures of sexual contact are poor tribute to its beauty, and as transient. The animal need to worship it is strong, often overpowering, but the animal act does not elevate. The worshipper debases himself and grovels because he is greater than his own or anyone else's body . . .

. . . Purple pensées at the pool . . .

Norfolk
Sun. 26th

To C of E service this morning . . . nostalgic, but it lacked the piquancy of a Catholic Mass.

My happiness fosters religious sentiment – though perhaps only as a defence against a worm of hopelessness niggling somewhere.

No idea who this cottage belongs to or what I'm doing here. Rufus inscrutable.

We sleep in the only bed though with no contact and, indeed, not too much desire. Enough is enough. Could pass the rest of my life like this. No! Gross naïvety to imagine that . . .

(I don't really care, but why does it have to be a fella? Everything'd be so simple if it wasn't a fella.)

. . . The selfishness of love . . .

Mon. 27th

Languid days. No work and have nothing to read but the delivered *Mirror*.

Drank all night on arrival then up at noon to sunny breakfast on the porch among humming bees and little bits of lacy patchy stuff, summer snow, floating in the sunlight leaking through the trees. Afternoons ambling lazily around the orchard and lying in long grass by the river smoking gear he calls 'kif' which is burnt in silver paper then rolled with tobacco.

Evenings to the village and the local where we drink with two Brummies. A parrot mocks 'You again!' whenever the saloon bar door opens.

Idyllic contentment. No need for words between us.

Near the weir children and young men fish and paddle from dawn to sunset. The water courses in a body, gently and solemnly like a religious procession. The weeds on the bed are long and green and nearly touch the surface, wavering splendidly for all the world like a woman's hair. Ducks paddle against the flow maintaining their exact positions. In the shallows a majestic, arrogant swan stands yawning its plumage. Three or four more float nearby, their necks lying coiled across their backs and their beaks like orange and black stones nesting in a basket of snow.

Beneath one of the bridges the legend 'I was sucked off by a twelve year old girl' is painted boldly in white. Astonishment is not at the message but that someone should find himself at that unlikely spot with paint-pot and brush.

All this juice and all this joy . . .

It spills down on me like the monsoons and wells up from a spring in my soul.

I am saturated.

Last night with the Brummies again. The four of us pretty pissed and outside, in a moment of good-will I kiss Phil (a giant but full of youthful reticence and wonder) lightly on the cheek. He is surprised though not displeased and both of them walk backwards waving the length of their street. Don't know how I get away with it.

Homing it along the haling path Rufus says 'You kissed that guy'.

I say 'Yes'.

'Why?'

'Guess I like kissing people I like.'

'You never kiss me.'

'I like *you* too much. Wouldn't trust myself.'

For the first time ever he laughs though I can only hear its music in the darkness. Then he says 'I know'.

Later, sprawled around the living-room here with a bottle of whisky and the light from the paraffin lamp dancing on our faces he spoke of himself with more candour and warmth than I'd thought him capable of . . .

Moments like that too precious, too impossible to transcribe . . .

If only he didn't have that obsession about wealth but, endearingly, it includes me. 'When I make my million Ke (he calls me Ke – like 'key') you and me's gunna relax. You and me's gunna go places, do things and we're not gunna give a goddam shit for nobody. We're brothers see.'

We finished the whisky. He made it to the bed but I must've flaked out on the settee. Still groggy this morning.

Driving off to find a pool. Or we might make it to the coast.

Wed. 29th

So bloody lazy. Hell of an effort even to scratch a few words in this notebook. Yet *now* is one time I'll want to remember.

It could never happen like this again.

Yarmouth crowded but a great lark idling on the beach and whooping it up in the water. Reckon we must have had about the best bronzies there.

Tremendous sensation of your own sexuality when you know it's being admired. Birds rallied round, often without encouragement. Took a couple of locals for a drive but didn't get anywhere beyond a bit of necking because one wouldn't come across for fear of the other.

Fucking silly gigglers anyway.

Drove back late and turned in tired. Rufus, casual as hell, says 'If you wanna put your arm around me Ke, go ahead'. I did and we slept like that and woke the same way. Generally I never sleep too peaceful.

My small world too sweet to last . . .

Soon a fool will hurl a stone and shatter the myth . . .

Probably me.

> Youth is a stranger hovering by
>   Dressed in my cast-off coat;
> Beauty's the echo sweet and shy
>   Of an unseen flautist's note;
> Time is a wind reaching down from the sky
>   Swelling the sails of the boat;
> 'Tack from the current' all three cry –
>   But my fingers have Love by the throat.

Thurs. 30th

Lying on lawn near door sunning and drinking beer which is too warm because we have no way of cooling it. Rufus in white trunks sits on steps which he calls a 'stoop' cleaning rifle. His concentration is profound. The proclivity of Americans for fire-arms. I wouldn't know what to do with the bloody thing . . .

Quarter of an hour watching centipede march across the lawn. It gets pretty stormy where the glades grow thick but he negotiates with dignity. He's not sure where he's going but he'd die rather than turn back. And he hasn't got a hundred legs, or so he tells me – they're manoeuvring appendages.

Discomfort of trying to write while lying on stomach. Little things bite and tickle and probe.

Rufus looks up from the gun and squints into the glare.

'What you doin'?'

I shrug. (It's pretty obvious what I'm doing.)

He says slowly, 'How much does a guy get for writing a book?'

'Depends. Abuse if it's any good . . . thousands if it's sick enough . . .'

He considers, then continues ramming the barrel.

Bet he's figuring out how to write a *very sick* book . . .

Looking around:

Woolly lambs scampering down a blue field of sky.

Twist and gnarl of ancient trees by the river.

Lushness of hedgerows and the inviting (thirst-quenching?) shade of the forest.

Quivering, darting rabbits. (Or hares or whatever they are.)

Tribes of insects sliding down sunbeams swamping the world. No noise. No traffic. The universe a cave of silence.

Glass-like opacity and sheer curve of water barrelling over the weir.

Skeleton of twelfth-century priory . . . its stones preserving a peace and spirituality which the weeds can't choke.

Beyond the door an 1889 calendar with days inked off till the middle of next month. (Ominous this; what terminated the markings . . . ?)

Rufus's eyes. The mould of his neck. His body, sweating as if with the pressure of its own beauty . . .

. . . A thousand things to note but am too voluptuously lazy . . .

Fri. 31st

Murmurs among the trees.
Leaf whispers it to leaf
And birds sing of it.

Birds wake the sun with their singing.
They fly into the sun's face as it rises
Chirping the secret.
The sun, scattering the darkness,
Revealing quiet corners,
Peers through windows to see if we know of it.

Do we know of it?

Fresh wells are tapped each successive creation.
New fountains leap to life
And gurgle of it streaming to join the waters.
Nature dances, writing it on petals.
She scatters the petals to the galaxies.

Can we read?

Home baked bread from a shop in the village.
Is there a world beyond Arcadia . . . ?

Sat. 1st

It's all going to finish tomorrow . . .
Went into the forest alone after breakfast and carved our names
on a tree.
When winter comes I'll return and find it and remember . . .
To an American Air Force Base last night with some Yanks we
picked up on the road. Wanted to like them for Rufus's sake but
they were shallow sort of, empty, false – I don't know.
Drank too much.

Driving back an ugly misshapen cloud nibbled at the moon and pretty soon it was devoured.

Sun. 2nd

Packing up.

Bit of a party here last night after the local. Dragged a few of the regulars round and Phil brought his guitar.

Ran out of booze and had to put the governor on the shake . . .

Good night altogether. Good songs. Wish I could sing.

After they'd gone he sort of half kissed me on the neck. He said 'When I make my money Ke it'll be like this all the time . . .'

Heart heavy as hell at leaving . . .

Mon. 3rd

Pete ringing as I get back. Wedding three weeks tomorrow. Pretty excited in a way – have never been to a wedding before. Pete says the grey suit'll be OK. Damned if I know what a best man's supposed to do but he says he'll find out from the vicar. Maybe they have a rehearsal or something . . .

Billie (or Jackie, I can never remember her name) says her old man's really lashing out – they're having over a hundred guests. Wonder if I can wangle an invite for Rufus; won't know anyone there except Fred and his missus and sister. Trouble is Pete doesn't like Rufus. Will try and right that tonight though . . .

(Court case on the 14th. Suspension of the licence hangs like a cloud over everything . . . already a grey day for the wedding.)

Livid with Guernsey. He asked me to recommend him for looking after the boiler. Apparently he showed up once but hasn't been seen since. Reverend Mother's been doing it herself. Feel bloody bad about it but she doesn't appear to be put out at all, just keeps asking if I had a good time and that makes it worse. Should've had more sense.

1830. Raining.

Rufus on his way round.

Inexplicably happy.

Agnes hurt that I went away without telling her. She thought I still had a cob on about the baby. Explained that Norfolk was a last-minute decision; said I'd rung but she wasn't home ... bloody phoney lie because she's always home.

Stopped the afternoon with her though – a session in the bed and then I did some odd jobs around the flat.

As from tomorrow I'm really going to get stuck into *Manicomio*. Don't care how awful it seems so far, am determined to complete at least a first draft.

Tues. 4th

Confused.

All mixed up ... I don't know, hurt I expect, and jealous. God knows, I've no reason to be.

Here's what happened: Last night, affectionate as hell. Sounds sloppy on paper but we've got something between us, Rufus and me, and it's precious ...

In the bunk we were lying there talking, no sex or anything (who needs it?) just talking, and he says 'You wanna stay clear of that faggot Ke, he's bad news.' (Rufus is picking up the English idiom.)

I thought he meant Pete and said 'No, you've got him wrong. He's my mate.'

'Not the guy who don't like me. He's OK. I mean the fag.' He meant Eugene.

'I'd piss on that creep.'

After a while he said 'He wants you to do faggy photographs'.

'How do you know that?'

'Don't you, Ke.'

'I'm not going to, but how do you know about it?'

'He told me.' (Hell, they only met for ten minutes.) 'Your buddies told me. They want me to talk you into doing them ... but I don't want you to, get me?'

(He was actually embarrassed. It was pretty beautiful to see.)

'Why? You in love with me or something?'

'Don't be goddam crazy. I like you, see. You're my buddy, see. I can talk to you. Generally speaking I can't talk to no one.' Silence for a while then he said, with indignation, 'Anyhow, I'm no queer'.

'I'm beginning to think *I* am.'

'You're crazy Ke. You ain't no queer. Shit man . . .'

'Well, why do you think I'm shacking up with you every night?'

'That's different! I'm beddin' down with you too, ain't I? . . . shit . . .'

Anyway that's the essence of it. We were pissed.

Surprise came this morning over coffee. We were sober again and him, nonchalant as ever, out of the blue says 'Did I tell you it was that faggot's cottage we were in?'

'Eh!'

'Yea! Thought I'd tell you before you heard it from the fag.'

I couldn't say anything. Inside me was all damp and icy stalactites of tears formed.

Driving me back in the motor he said 'I'm sure glad we went Ke. I got to know you. Now I'd go for nothin'.' And afterwards 'You stay clear of that fag Ke. He's after assin' you about.'

. . . Shit I love you Rufus baby. I can't think or eat or any fucking thing. It's weak as hell but all my guts goes crying after you . . .

Lunch-time. Wonder how much Eugene paid Rufus to take me to Norfolk and what Horror Face expected to gain out of it.

Have tried and tried but can't apply myself to writing fiction. It's bewildering but words are flaccid and meaningless unless they give theatre to my feelings.

Read an A. E. Coppard story *Marching to Zion*. So lovely it saddened me.

Too dull to swim this afternoon and I don't want to go to Agnes's because we're taking Penny and her mate to dinner.

Excuse for another jump. At least it saves us from knocking each other off . . .

Pete even more at loggerheads with Rufus last night, probably because he's a Yank. Pete's got a thing about Yanks. He openly abused him once or twice but Rufus remained impervious.

Kind of funny because I love them both, in different ways . . .

It's me who feels the pain . . .

Eugene so sickening in Knightsbridge it hardly bears mentioning.

Think I'll just lie down and think. Get all sexed up about tonight perhaps.

Wed. 5th

Father Michael, Reverend Mother and another nun here when Rufus strolled in. He was shy of their costumes. They were all taken with him. The atmosphere was good.

They were over about Mrs Grey's jewels to ask if she'd ever shown them to me or mentioned them or anything. (She hadn't, of course.) Apparently the Hong Kong daughter is talking of police and lawyers and the Convent doesn't want a scandal. They believe, and I'm inclined to agree with them, that there never were any jewels or that if there were Mrs Grey got rid of them years ago.

Father Michael stayed on after the nuns had gone to charm Rufus and, I suspect, to see what gives between us. It was Rufus who charmed him by being his matter-of-fact self.

Father Michael is shrewd though. His eyes took a cardiograph and he was mildly bemused . . .

Half an hour late at Penny's last night and they still weren't ready.

Took them to a decent Hungarian place near Barking where they drank too much wine (all to our purpose) then to a club in Forest Gate where they drank too much gin (which clinched the deal . . . not that there was any doubt it was in the market anyway).

Fucking great it was too! Penny writhed and groaned and sweated and put the scissors on as if to squeeze a nation out of me.

Came my dust three times last night and twice this morning. Don't think Rufus did as well. After we'd dropped the girls off this morning he said to me 'Don't never again try tellin' me you're thinkin' of turnin' queer'.

I said 'Oh, my body's OK. It's my mind. Half the time I was thinking of you.'

He sort of grinned noncommittally and I could have kicked myself. It wasn't even true. It was just the fact that he was alongside immersed in his own pleasure that gave a fullness to mine . . .

How can I explain that without sounding wishy-washy . . . ?

Anyway it was about the best bang-off I've ever had (though I daren't tell Agnes that). And wonderfully relaxing too, no matter what the theologians say. Feel ripe for *Manicomio*.

1815. Telegram:

FLYING TUNIS BACK FRI/SAT RUFUS

Told you he was tight fisted . . . look at that for economy. (Actually he's been pretty liberal moneywise since we went to Norfolk.)

Friday's a million light years away and Saturday's veiled in eternity . . .

Still, I guess I'll muckle through.

Manicomio all afternoon and it spills from the pen with no effort.

Began to clip the hedges round the common this evening but the old dears kept getting in the way. Baited them a bit; they're a giggle when you start them off.

Wish Pete would ring or I had some way of contacting him.

No mind for more work. Will do the locals.

Thurs. 6th

Finished up in the West End last night.

Bars empty without Rufus and even the beer was insipid. Hope he makes it back tomorrow. It's only a few hours' flight.

Guernsey in the Lion. Abused him for letting me down as regards the boiler. Abuse useless; he's impervious to anything that has no foundation in his fantasies. He did afford an explanation though – he'd forgotten he'd promised to accompany a millionaire to Paris . . .

At that point I gave up and drank round with him a while . . .

Came back and stayed the night with Agnes. Her appetite for fellatio is becoming insatiable . . . I feel like a pump . . .

Raining so I can't carry on with the hedge.

1900. Eight hours straight writing, writing. My arm's dropping off and my neck's cricked.

One day it's all going to stop, mid-sentence, mid-thought; no climax, no time to tie up the loose ends; no punctuation . . .

Depression and a sort of fear, and a longing for Rufus.

> Loves there are like snakes which coiled lie
> To writhe and rear in the hearts of men;
> To flash off venom from a fondling eye
> And poison bodies while caressing them . . .

Is my affection evil? (surely not!) or good? (but there's *something* wrong) or does the balance of the scales depend on me?

Either way it's hopeless. I'm imprisoned in a body which is locked and bolted from the outside, and the need for escape gnaws at me . . . escape to another prison or share my own . . . it's the isolation that terrifies . . .

The need, the need, the urgent need . . . is there nothing but suicide to end it? Oh but even then I suspect the isolation would carry over into permanency. The need is saturated with the eternal. Any lover will confirm that.

Is whatever influence I have on Rufus against his interest? I thought at first he was a seasoned cynic but that hardy husk fronts for an exploring innocence and a measure of immaturity . . .

Perhaps he sees me in the same light . . .

In a way isn't that everybody . . .

Oh bollocks to analysis!

Fri. 7th

No Rufus yet.

Time stands alert and motionless like an arched cat.

It's after mid-day but a pre-dawn silence pervades the room. Any moment I expect the telephone to cock-crow, and the sun will rise. Twice already I've leapt as its alarm has shattered the silence. First it was Penny whining for a return match, then it was the actor purring about last night . . .

It's good to feel wanted but it hurts like hell to want.

Daren't leave the room.

Was swirled about in the eddies of Soho last night and later washed up at Knightsbridge. The lads were there; Tony all wit and hilarity, Tom drunk and slightly surly. Geoff arrived just after me all fresh from a job; he related its incidents in detail.

All asked for Rufus and Peter.

Was going on with them to the club for old times' sake but the actor came into the boozer so I went back to his place. Drank brandy and played records. Screwed him (£10) then we had a hell of a good conversation about writers and poets and he was all a-dither because I hadn't read *Death in Venice* and he gave me his copy. Read it this morning and was quite stunned.

Nothing to do but read. *Peter Abelard*, Helen Waddell. Some sections point straight to the eternal.

1500. No phone. Perhaps he's coming on a later plane.

2100. Busting myself up sitting here. Going to seek escape in the ministrations of Agnes. Leaving phone off hook. If he rings he'll think it's engaged and know I'm about.

Sat. 8th

Insomnia, but without the fears.

Switched the radio off when Luxembourg closed down and stared at my book-spines crystallised in the yellow glare from the street lamps till dawn . . .

Feel patient and loving like a martyr. Would even do my executioners a good turn so sweet and gentle and smug I feel.

Consolation is that Rufus'll definitely be back today, Saturday.

Wish he'd come in now. Just tip-toe in or something, no need for words, just sit down or something and be around . . .

(Tadzio! Tadzio! . . .)

Of course he might have arrived late and not rung in case he woke me.

Guess he'll ring when he's ready.

1642. Grappled with *Manicomio* all morning. Good work considering but had to get out of the room after lunch.

Went to the Oasis. Splashed around in the pool, dodging bodies, then stretched out on the sun-deck, down by the far wall where Rufus and me usually lie . . .

(Phoned every half hour or so but no answer.)

Alongside, so close he was almost hugging me, a beautiful Eurasian kid. Very shy but he eventually opened a conversation. Said he'd seen me there before. Said he'd always wanted to talk but thought I might hit him. Asked if I was married. When I was showering he came in and ran his fingers timidly down my chest and muttered something about me being handsome. *That* couldn't go unrewarded so took him to Picture Hat's club, mostly to witness her horror at his colour. Not so. Apparently his cuddliness appealed to her and she took him to her maternal bosom . . . squashed him to death as likely as not. I don't know; had one drink and cabbed home.

Midnight. To the Classic with Agnes to see one of AG's old movies. Where does all that glamour and dramatic power go to off screen?

Agnes held my hand. I was irritated by the contact, itching almost, and the pressure she exerted asked questions. Wanted to withdraw mine but didn't dare – the callousness might bounce back on me from Rufus.

Sometimes I feel I really hate her . . .

Simulated affection and later gave her the works in bed. Thought I'd excelled myself until she said 'I love *you*, Keiron – you yourself. You don't have to pretend with me . . .'

Women have a hypersensitive intuition.

Wonder if she knows . . .

No Rufus yet though I've just rung again.

Looks like another sleepless night. Father Michael saw my light and came in. Hoped he would stay for a drink but he's got an early call and is off to Cheshire. Would like to have talked to him about Rufus . . . but perhaps wiser not.

You're the only one I can tell things to, Journal. You and God . . . and Eddie if he was still alive.

Marooned in a vast night and sleep, the rescuer, won't come.

Nothing for it but the kif . . .

. . . Tranquil, alert and mellow . . .

Rufus flutters around me like a fledgling.

I love him – which is a bloody irrational statement for a start because

> I don't know who I am
> Or what love is
> Or who he is

but I love him anyway and do you know how I can tell? I can tell by the paradoxes like for instance I want to cry but I won't because that's sickening so I won't cry which is impossible and everything's like that and I'm chasing my tail all day long.

You're more than a friend Rufus . . . you're father-mother-brother-sister-guardian angel-and-Santa Claus. You are closer than life's blood and dearer than youth. I'd do myself an injury sooner than see you wronged mate, die if I had to . . .

130

... Fuck you Rufus, you're choking me; can't you see you're choking me? I want to be left alone. Alone and free ... free like Carmen ... but I haven't got the guts ... I'm hardly a man any more ... racing like the Gadarene swine to my own destruction ...

Rufus — what sort of fool name's that anyhow? Sounds like a dog.

No, a rich name really. Redolent of Viking warriors, or a Latin goat-herd perhaps fluting to wood nymphs from green pastures ... with a hey nonny nonny ...

(Rufus the Red! Splendid old sodomite! Didn't give a damn ...)

... *Say, I don't give a sheeet man. You know what I want? I want we're alone somewhere, Ke, just alone, you an' me, in a windmill, igloo or sumpin' ... under the ground say, yea, in a coffin with a blank headstone, just the two of us, no need for talkin' man, nothin' wild, just sort of ... I dunno ... anythin' ...*

We're twins ...

Cheers baby, you've got your script right.

... *No kiddin', big things are comin' my way an' we're gonna share 'em. Get me? A cool million an' you an' me's in Tahiti or wherever, livin' man, livin' high an' playin' native an' sheet man, we's gonna be happy ...*

Rosy days yonder, eh, old visionary.

Forget it!

We're dead, understand? Dead! Shrouded together, coffined, six feet under. We're decaying, stinking, crumbling. Quiet baby, watch the worms, slowly, steady. See how our limbs rust at the hinges and drop off; see how we cave in one on another till your dust is indistinguishable from my dust and the great union is complete.

Passion mocking itself ...

Sun. 9th

What the hell was that all about? He doesn't even talk like that. And it was so laden with cabbalistic significance under the kif last night.

Doldrums! Off wandering ...

131

1800. Footsore and a rotten headache.

Walked for miles through city, Fleet Street, Strand, West End and Embankment. Phoned from every booth. Got maudlin drunk in an appalling boozer in Earl's Court full of middle-aged perverts in leather jackets and studded belts (wonder what homely jobs they do during the week). Must have been chatted up by a dozen of them and each time the horror of eventually joining their doomed band engulfed me and produced a sort of self-pitying despair which made me morose and that seemed to attract them all the more ; . . .

Slept off the booze at Agnes's. Her wan worshipful smile infuriates me but her fingers soothe.

Just now Reverend Mother comes to the boiler and is a fountain of giggles over something which evinces too mild an acknowledge-ment from me. She walks with me as far as the rose-garden and expresses concern . . . I'm not the same young man, etc. I beat about a bit then, hypocrite, say 'Woman trouble!' Her eyes dance. 'Ah, I thought as much,' and she winks and wags her finger and nods her head sagely.

At that moment I could have switched allegiance and fallen in love with her . . .

Springy waltz on the radio. It depresses me so much I get a sort of masochistic pleasure out of leaving it on.

Rufus . . . Rufus . . . Rufus . . .

I am a harp. His name, eyes, grin, inapprehensible beauty swirl like fresh winds from a warm place plucking sweet mournful notes from the fibres of my being.

That's crap! How about:

Name, eyes and things dripping around me invisibly, like dew, and the morning finding the vapours condensed on me, coursing sweat-like off my skin.

Oh hell Rufus, come back won't you; for fuck's sake come back . . .

You and me have no people and that night we promised to be brothers – remember?

SURVIVAL

It was hot in the hatch, hot and clammy, and Colin wore his tiredness like a greatcoat.

His ears were deafened by the roar of the air hose and his eyes, red and swollen behind the goggles, swam in a sea of billowing grain dust. His mouth was covered by a surgeon's mask yet it didn't really keep the dust out and the taste in his mouth was like burnt porridge. Still, these things didn't matter, they were nothing compared with his tiredness. It was like a drug. If he hadn't been so tired he couldn't have kept going at all.

He scoured the surfaces with the air hose and bent its nozzle into every pocket, scattering the yellow pellets. The others followed up with brooms sweeping the lot onto the level below, then waiting till half the deck was pulled back on the tension wires and they'd scramble down and repeat the operation. There were six double car-decks like that in six double hatches, and cleaning them down after a bulk cargo was a hellish work-up. You wouldn't find anyone doing it shore-side – not for ten bob an hour anyway but somehow you stuck it, somehow it made you feel part of something and even if you kicked you knew that being part of that something was a reward you couldn't put a price to.

When they finally reached the bottom deck of Number 6 it was midnight. If bells were still rung it would have been eight bells but now you just called it midnight. Shore gangs were working along the hatches behind them, hosing down and hauling out drums of gash with the cranes. They'd be finished in two hours and tugs and pilot had been ordered to take the ship up the river for loading.

Colin climbed the forty rungs of the hatch access ladder, along the tunnel and up into the accommodation. In his cabin he didn't dare sit down. Moving like a man underwater he took off his clothes and left them in a heap in a corner. In the shower-room he stood for a long while as the jets sluiced the

133

dust from his limbs and soothed like the fingers of a masseur.

The bosun leaned into the shower-room. 'You'll be on the wheel when we get away, all right?'

He'd forgotten what watch he was on. He'd been working with few breaks for thirty-six hours. It hardly mattered. 'OK' he said. 'I'll be on the after deck.' If he turned in now he'd never wake up.

The cook was in the alleyway when he came out of the shower-room. Colin saw but didn't notice his glazed lurching. The cook said 'You want that hair-cut now son?'

'OK.' It'd help pass the time.

'I'll fetch the gear.'

Colin slipped into a pair of jeans and a T-shirt. He was towelling his hair when an impulse drew him to the port box. He pulled back the curtains and unscrewed the lugs of his square port window. He pushed it open.

He was startled by a sensation, as sudden and as absurd as the wail of a banshee, that something was going to happen that night.

He leaned his elbows in the box and gazed down a level onto the after deck as he dried his hair. From that angle the after deck looked more like a stage-set in a theatre. Night hung as curtains but the centre was well lighted and a yellowish glow showed where the sky was. A thin gauze of wheat dust rippling over the scene conveyed an air of unreality, or rather of theatrical reality, as if raw life had been condensed to a two hour stint and was being enacted here.

The atmosphere was charged with an electricity. Plays move inexorably towards climaxes.

Mooring ropes ran taut from the bits to the bollards on the quay where rats slunk around the base of the huge silos, rising like the columns of an ancient ruin, solid against the sky. A bulk carrier flying the same flag as themselves lay stern to stern with them and beyond her to port the sea was a dark jelly all the way to the breakwater.

Everyone seemed to have gathered there, on the poop. The stewards had been ashore for a last run and had returned with a crowd from the bulk carrier. They'd brought tables and chairs out of the bar and were determined to enjoy themselves. Cases of beer lay torn open on the deck and cans passed from hand to hand. A record-player told of love and the loneliness of prison. Men laughed and swore at each other. It was all in the script.

The sailors who were too tired to change after their long hours in the hatches had removed their overalls and were lying on the deck or sitting stretched out with their heads and shoulders propped against the bulwarks. Two men were fishing over the seaward side, a fireman, patiently with a line, and Dansk using a net full of scraps of meat which fooled greenish-grey crabs as big as soup plates every five minutes. When they were hauled up they were flung, writhing, into galvanised buckets.

It occurred to Colin that the lives of humans were no less precarious than the lives of the creatures below . . .

There was a knock on the door and the cook fumbled his way in. Colin pushed the mat to one side and slid the chair into the centre. He set the towel around his shoulders as he sat down.

'How do you want it?'

'Not too short; you know . . . '

'You look tired son.'

'I'm knackered,' said Colin.

The cook, who was flexing his clippers, stopped abruptly. He looked indignant at first, then almost hurt. When he spoke it was in a quiet voice, but firm, spiced with a sort of mad authority. 'That's no word to use son; don't you know Jesus hears every word you say . . . ?'

Colin thought dully 'The cook's been drinking'.

He didn't dare close his eyes. Sleep beguiled, mocked him like a whore in a doorway. He sat hunched forward in the chair as the cool steel wriggled up and down his neck like an inquisitive lizard and shot charges of sensual pleasure along the tired sinews of his back and arms. Goose pimples formed on his skin.

It's pretty pleasant, he thought, pretty relaxing.

' . . . God gave His Only Begotten Son . . . '

Snippets of hair tickled as they fell on his bare arms. Music filtered up from the poop. Colin thought, 'Being knackered can have its compensations. I feel like I've been on the weed.'

The cook placed the clippers on the table and took up his

comb and scissors. 'The wages of sin is death' he announced, holding the scissors upright, parallel to Colin's ear. 'We are sinners son, sinners all. Jesus alone saves . . .'

'Not too much off the top Bill; I don't care for it too short.'

'Stand up, stand up for Jesus
Ye soldiers of the cross . . .'

Colin's immediate impulse was to stand up. He tried to ignore the cook's Jesusing but that wasn't easy. He had to admit it embarrassed him but he couldn't tell why. He felt like a child who sees a parent naked.

'Lift high His Royal Banner,
Ye shall not suffer loss.'

It wasn't the same Jesus Colin knew. He was like your own thoughts about people, your daydreams, your animal fantasies. You kept those things to yourself – wrestled with them, worshipped them, hated them according to the season of your mind. You understood them knowing that you didn't understand them or perhaps you just couldn't explain them, or nobody would understand you if you could or something like that but anyway you kept them to yourself . . .

It wasn't even the same Jesus.

Jan passed in the alleyway then doubled back.

'Hey Col! Let me have a couple of thousand yen? You'll get it back next sub.'

'In the top drawer. What's up?'

'Pornies,' Jan said. He motioned down the alleyway and a little Japanese slipped into the cabin. Jan took two notes from the drawer. The Japanese unbuttoned his shirt and drew out a pile of magazines. 'From Sweden,' he said. 'Very much dirty girl. OK?'

The cook made a sound that wasn't quite a groan and wasn't quite a shriek. His face grew very red. The Japanese, imagining the cook to be overwhelmed by lust, made a slight bow in his direction and smiled courteously.

Jan fingered quickly through the books and selected two. 'A thousand each Col,' he said. 'You can make a bomb on these, some ports. They're an investment.'

With a cry of 'Filth!' the cook flung the comb and scissors on to the deck and made a lunge at the books in Jan's hand. But Jan was too agile; he leapt back into the alleyway where he stood in an attitude of mock fear, laughing hugely.

'Filth!' cried the cook again. 'Sin and shame and filth!' Then, with a magnificent howl of 'Antichrist!' he whacked the astounded Japanese clean across the face with the remaining literature.

There was a scuffle after that which was dominated by Jan's laugh. Colin held his head in his hands and asked himself where people got the energy. Presently he got up and removed the towel from his shoulders. In the alleyway Jan was baiting the cook with graphic descriptions of the photos in his books. The cook himself knelt in perfervid prayer holding the rest of the books aloft as if expecting God to reach down and borrow them. The little Japanese hugged the bulkhead waiting for an opportunity to retrieve his stock.

Colin squeezed past them and walked down the ladder to the poop.

''Ere Col, who cut your 'air?'

'Jesus.'

''Asn't half made a mess.'

'Isn't finished. He was called off to preach somewhere.' They laughed. Jesus was always good for a laugh.

Colin took a seat at one of the tables with the stewards and the crowd off the bulk carrier. Someone offered him a beer. He shook his head but the beer was thrust at him and he took it. It was pointless telling men who'd been drinking that you didn't want to drink. They were on a different wavelength.

There was much talk but Colin didn't listen. Fatigue still hung on his limbs like wet clothing and he didn't feel inclined to speak.

His mind drifted. Someone sang a song and he thought 'I'm on stage'. He was conscious again that a play was in building here, that all these commonplaces were going to culminate in some important, perhaps staggering event.

Destiny was herding them, drawing them towards a momentous *something*.

It was a crazy notion and he dismissed it for the second time. It was easier to yield to lassitude.

When the talk was loudest the Captain came down the ladder with the Chief Engineer and two guests. As soon as they were aware of the Captain's presence the lads hushed. The lads off the bulk carrier were told, 'That's the Old Man' and they too fell silent. The group had to walk among the silence to reach the gangway.

Suddenly, violently, Colin thought 'What a load of bullshit!' He thought 'Why can't the lads act natural?'; they make the bastards think they're some kind of Royalty.' He wanted to stand up and shout his contempt, to cut down that conceited snob, the Chief Engineer; he wanted to commit some obscenity to shock the shore-siders who looked at *the men* as zoo-strollers look at caged savagery.

He was surprised at the intensity of his own hatred.

The silence spotlighted the Captain's rank but he was a modest man and carried it awkwardly. He flushed and grinned and asked quickly 'Somebody's birthday?'

When the group were out of earshot the talk started again, bolder and more self-confident than before. Someone said that the Old Man was a gentleman and that he took an interest in the lads. The one whom Colin always thought of as the snivelling geezer said that if the Old Man was all that concerned why didn't he come down the hatches and lend a hand? None of them up there ever did a stroke, he said.

Colin's blood caught fire and razed his old resolution not to be put out by the snivelling geezer. He spat an obscenity at him. 'The Mate's been grafting along with the best,' Colin said. 'It's you that's the lazy bastard; yea you! As far as the rest of us are concerned we're a man short on deck . . . '

The snivelling geezer defended himself energetically but Colin wasn't listening. He despised the snivelling geezer for a two-faced bum. A fella could slave himself twenty-five hours a day for months but if he went adrift once or got pissed once or opened his mouth once he was branded as unreliable and stood in the stocks till pay-off. But you'd never catch the snivelling geezer at tricks like that. He hadn't the imagination. His only instinct was self-preservation, his only recreation moaning. He was a slug. And yet they thought the world of him upstairs. He was always on the job, they said. It didn't seem to matter that he did nothing when he got there, he was always reliable . . .

Stuff it, so was death!

Jan strolled out from the housing and crouched down on the deck beside Colin's chair. He was grinning mischievously and he still held his purchases.

Colin said 'What you done with Jesus?'

Jan said ' 'E's got the Nip in 'is cabin fillin' 'im with booze an' Bible. Poor Nip can't tell wot 'e's on about; keeps tryin' to flog 'im pornies. It's a circus, I can tell you . . . '

Colin took one of the books and the crowd off the bulk carrier fought as they scrambled for the other. They turned the pages with a slow hunger, mocking and gloating in turn. The next page always held a promise which it never quite fulfilled.

Colin thought cynically 'When you've seen one of these you've seen the lot', but as he leafed through he couldn't quell the urgent sensation which stirred, at first, then all but paralysed his body. His mind was possessed by an uninhibited abandon. He'd wallow in any of the models' activities – grovel, lick, yield himself . . . no, he wanted to conquer, he wanted to tower over thighs and breasts, kneading, grinding them into submission. Fantasy built castle upon castle among higher and higher clouds while his mind and body, too tired to resist, screamed with the agony . . .

As Colin tossed the book on the table (with a non-committal grunt) Jan asked no one in particular 'Say, how does a fella go about getting a job like that . . . ?'

Someone said ' 'Ere, I just thought – see this Swede with the hairy arse, 'e don't half look like Jesus. Wonder if . . . '

One of the crowd off the bulk carrier asked, 'Who's this Jesus anyway?' and Jan told him.

'It's only when he's pissed,' he explained.

The fellow on the bulk carrier said, 'Our Taff's got a song finishes up like that; not quite like that, something like that. Give us that "Freighterman's Song" Taff.'

The one called Taff ummed and aahed and took a long swig of beer. Then he sang:

'You call us drunken bums
An' the scruffiest o' scums
As you sit about an' sip your soda-ed gins;
But you haven't gotta notion
Of the life upon the ocean
An' the way it makes for bawdy sorta sins.'

The song had a full-throated, roller coaster tune but threading through it, linked perhaps by the lower notes, ran strains of melancholy and gruff rebellion which found echoes in the heart.

'Have you ever roared ashore
For a night on Singapore
To whoop it up an' tell 'em who you are?
Have you ever met with Satan
Corked inside a bottle waitin'
On a table in a Bugis Strasse Bar?

Have you ever done a spreader
When they've sprung a double-header
On y'u, packin' gear an' cleanin' down y'r shelves?
Have y'u seen the bastards bog y'u
When they've 'ad y'u up to log y'u
An' you've told them sundry facts about themselves?

Have you yeared it on a tanker
In a cold an' lonely wanker
A-dreamin' of the comfort of a kiss?
Have you saved up all your earnin's
An' your feelin's an' your yearnin's
For a prostitute who only takes the piss?

Have you ever known a bosun
Who could punch your fuckin' nose in
Then booze you up an' never tell you why?
That was Ginger Mick McCraunin
An' 'e 'anged 'imself this mornin'.
(Have you ever found you've guts enough to cry?)

Now we don't give a monkey's
About you Jesus-junkies
An' your padres sound so phoney when they spout;
But *you* might find more in it
If you pause to think a minute
That He picked His mates from fellas shippin' out . . .

Jan said 'Hey! Give us that again, I didn't catch it all,' but the
record-player was on again playing its only record which told
of love and the loneliness of prison and the one Taffy was
throwing back another can of beer.

Colin's eyes persisted in falling shut. The excitement which
had so racked his body moments before had cooled and he had
forgotten it. He hadn't touched his drink but now he swallowed
half of it hoping that it might fend off the sleep which threatened
to swamp him.

Dansk, fishing in the wings, called 'Hey!' and beckoned
across the deck with an upraised arm. The rest of his body was
leaning over the bulwark peering into the water. Several
wandered towards him saying 'What's up?' or 'What is it?' and
their sudden exclamations brought the others flocking to the
side.

Colin moved with them, urged more by the need to keep
awake than by curiosity. He edged between two bodies and
looked down into the water below. A shark glided just beneath
the surface. It was twice as big as a man and its arrogance was
splendid.

Someone called 'Fetch a cluster', and when one was found it
was let down on its own lead to hang there, a foot above the
water. The surface of the sea reflected the bulbs as a mirror and
the immediate world of the giant was lit up like an aquarium.

The shark was curious about the light. He wove round and
round in circles, his sleek fin slicing the water and his awesome
flesh snaking with terrible symmetry.

The lads tossed down a crab from the bucket. The smack as it
hit the water knocked it out and it sank like a stone. The shark
ignored it.

Someone raced to the galley and returned with a shoulder of

thawing meat. They stuck the meat with a butcher's hook and lowered it into the sea alongside the cluster. They juggled it about. Blood like whisps of smoke curled into the water and immediately the shark was alert. He approached with the single-mindedness of a warship and circled as if waiting for orders.

For almost five minutes he circled, mesmerising the lads who watched. It was like a sacrificial ritual with the pilot fish dancing in attendance. Without warning he halted. Then there was a deadly second before he swung round and lunged in the direction of the bait. The lads quickly tugged at the line and the shark leapt clear of the water. He somersaulted but the swing of the line deceived his aim, and he missed his mark.

'You could've 'ad 'im, you nutter. Let 'im take it, let 'im take it . . . '

When the water settled he was still there prowling ominously, excited by the smell of the blood.

They lowered the bait again. It was hardly in the water before the shark, with one incredible thrust of his streamlined body, soared up and lifted it neatly from the hook. It all happened so suddenly that the lads hadn't time to register. All they saw was the flash of a milk white belly slashed by the serrated crescent of a mouth.

He cruised for the best part of a minute, proudly, contemptuously, power rippling the length of his majestic body and lingering in the sea long after he'd turned and spiralled down into the dark well beneath.

A flying fish, zig-zagging in panic, scudded towards the light. It was airborne for several seconds before it collided with the ship's side. The whack of the encounter had barely sounded when a pursuing porpoise, with speed and effortless precision, snapped its jaws over the stunned flyer. It hadn't even time to flop back into the water.

Shoals of tiny nervous arrows darted into the aquarium as one body, stood rigid, then danced statically as if electrocuted by the light.

Other fish appeared; mullet appeared, eels appeared, cat-fish with glum faces appeared, all wandering in from the rim of darkness and hovering around to inspect the phenomenon of the light. Little things, jelly-fish with tentacles, soft and mushy, which vanished when the lads tried to focus drifted just beneath the surface and insects with wings like whirling skirts wrote hieroglyphics on the sea-top.

The shrill demands of a telephone in the housing broke the silence. Presently the bosun stepped out onto the deck.

'Fore and aft,' he called. 'Get the gangway clear of the quay first.' To Colin he said 'The pilot's on the bridge'.

Colin said 'OK' and started off up the deck ladders. His weariness pressed on him more heavily than ever now but he was getting used to it. In fact he scarcely gave it a thought. Burdens were no longer burdens once you got used to them. They became part of routine and you bore them effortlessly like you bore the weight of your own body and the gaze of God.

The funnel deck was in darkness. Crossing to starboard he followed the rails with his hand to avoid the swimming-pool. He paused mid-ships to look down onto the after deck. It was deserted now; the actors had left the stage. The props were all in position but props are only shadows of ghosts without actors.

Colin experienced a deep sense of emptiness, of unfulfilment. Nothing had been resolved. He'd been tricked and the worst of it was – it was he himself who'd done the tricking . . .

Though perhaps something not immediately discernible *had* occurred, something that needed to be hatched in the mind before its full significance could be absorbed. Perhaps the climax had been in symbols – in the Jesusing, in the haircut, in Jan's vulnerable innocence hiding behind his good looks and veneer of worldliness; in the sexual thing; in the tiredness . . .

Colin laughed slightly, as a thief does when he's caught red-handed. What the hell had he expected? Murder? Love? Apotheosis?

Life isn't a play. At best it's a game of football, amateur and with few supporters. You take the field in the beginning and learn your skills as you play. The opponent is always more experienced than you and it takes everything you have to stay on the defensive. The score stands at an unvarying nil-all and there's no stopping until the referee blows his whistle.

On the bridge the pilot said to Colin 'Easy to port. Stop.

Midships. Stop. Easy to port. Stop. When she's in the stream just keep her head on that radio tower. The river's straight enough – it's the current that's tricky . . . '

Mon. 10th

Is this mad emotional stampede making me neurotic? I don't know. I've no gauge; there's been no precedent in my experience. I think I was a reasonably steady sort of fella before.

I'll tell you, I would have hammered Rufus last night . . .

Nothing mattered, regrets could wait; after more than I was going to take I was up and ready to swing and it was Tom who stopped me. He just grabbed my bollocks from behind and pulled me down so I was sitting on his forearm then he squeezed and it hurt like fuck which did nothing for my temper but when I turned on him he wore such a wry expression that my thoughts conflicted and I wasn't too sure what had happened. He took the fist I held ready and drew it beneath the table (the others couldn't see) clapped it over his crotch and held it there with his hand.

I started to laugh. I couldn't help it. Nerves I suppose, but anyway it *was* pretty funny.

So when I started laughing so did everybody else and I laughed the harder because no one but Tom and me knew exactly what had happened. Then at exactly the right time, when the threat of a fight had passed, he disengaged his hand, and mine, and I'll tell you that fella shot up in my estimation one hundred per cent.

At first Rufus had thought I was serious (which I was) but when I started laughing he took it to be a joke, a way of saying 'cool it down' and I could feel his heart rush out to me (had Tom's animal judgement seen that too?) and after that he was his insouciant self. Before we left Knightsbridge he said 'You're comin' back tonight ain't you Ke?' I told him yea, OK, and he slipped me his key saying he had business but would be home in a couple of hours.

Cabbed to Russell Square and turned in. Woke this morning 0600. No Rufus. What gives . . . ?

Here with Rufus all day . . .

He's unrecognisable as the cool self-confident draft-dodger in dark glasses I met at the pool that first afternoon. People are like parcels in a way, neatly boxed and strung, handsomely stamped and well addressed, pregnant with promise. To reveal their mysteries you've got to pry them open – and they're never what you expect. Rufus is no exception, but no disappointment either. I expected a stone, or marble at best. Found an uncut diamond . . .

He's been strangely affectionate and confiding today, misty almost, and even revealed flashes of humour.

His honesty is peculiar. I mean, he's utterly guileless when it comes to lying or stealing yet the same guilelessness carries him through the Customs' sheds with God knows how much heroin or cocaine or whatever sort of dope it is he fetches in.

He's not ashamed of his affection either, a bit surprised maybe, but he accepts it with the same sort of reverence an illiterate might a well-bound book. It doesn't occur to him that I mightn't feel the same way about him . . . or are his emotions simply a response to mine?

. . . His sincerity in wanting to protect me while wanting to be protected himself. It mirrors my own confusion. Says he told Eugene he *won't let* me do 'photographs or any of that shit' yet in the same breath he hopes I don't mind him making a few bucks off the old faggots while it's around.

He can't understand why I won't pack up and move into Russell Square with him. Neither can I except that it would be imprudent at this stage.

I was rash the other night. I exaggerated the whole thing.

What happened was: he cabled from Tunis what time to expect him Heathrow Friday. Of course I wasn't there (I got no cable) so he delivered the goods and went on the booze. He thought I was making a cunt of him. The more he thought about it, he said, the worse it became and when I strolled into Knightsbridge with Guernsey and more or less ignored him all his bitterness surfaced.

I said, 'Hell, if I couldn't say anything it was because I was so pleased to see you. I never felt so lost and miserable in my life as those days you were, away. I was crossing off the hours as that much living wasted.' Then I asked him what he was doing between Friday and Sunday.

Apparently when he was half pissed he rang Eugene who, predictably, had been pestering him since he consented to Norfolk.

Eugene put him out to stud in Gallaby's with some geezer (bet it was the Froggie) who tried to get stuck up him. He acted the scene out and that slow drawl of his and the lurch of his way of walking were pretty comical.

He said 'I felt so damn awful foolish Ke, I couldn't even get hard. Here's me standin' in this room and this guy's on his knees openin' my pants. I'm tryin' to look as if I don't notice but sheet man, you can't, and I'm tryin' to think what to do with my hands 'cause they're danglin' everywhere so I put 'em in my pockets and my damn pants fell down. Then this guy gets my prick out an' I'm fuckin' embarrassed Ke, 'cause it looks so small, like a li'l carrot or sumpin' an' he starts jerkin' an' suckin' at it an' it just shrinks like it's frightened and here's me sweatin' like I dunno what . . .

'Then he tells me to lie on the bed an' I do an' he turns the lights out an' peels my clothes off an' licks me down like a cat, which wasn't too bad but it made me feel kinda sick and anyway I was still slack as hell an' I was gonna tell him to leave it awhile an' next I know he's halfway up my ass . . . man did I bolt! You never saw no one get out of a goddam room so smart.'

(I asked if it was the first time he'd been with a geezer. 'Yea – 'cept in school. There was this guy we used to call Swoop 'cause that's all he ever did . . . a regular cocksucker, all day if you gave him the chance. There were a horny lotta fellas in that place too so you can guess he was kept mighty busy. Nice guy he was. Kinda quiet. Sick I guess. They put him in a loony house after a while . . . ')

Seems he continued to binge after that and spent the night with a whore in Lancaster Gate. Eugene leased him out again the next afternoon which earned an easy fifteen quid because all the fella wanted to do was look at Rufus and wank himself. Then another night in Gallaby's and he'd settled comfortably into the industry.

I say 'Four fellas in as many days with no previous experience. You've got a calling baby.'

'It's the money Ke,' he says with intense seriousness. 'I don't even talk to them.'

In the boozer during the lunch-time session he detailed his sexual history. There wasn't much to it really, as furtive as anybody else's and as meaningless. He confided that he rarely masturbates. 'Don't do nothin' for me,' he said.

At one point there was a broadcast about Robert Service with some good readings which moved Rufus more than I would have thought. They didn't do 'The Call of the Wild' so afterwards I recited it for him and he said 'Sheet Ke, that's great, I mean really great. You wanna give me that stuff when I'm goin' to sleep . . . that's when that stuff's best . . . ' He thought he'd betrayed a weakness and stared sheepishly at the ceiling.

'Yea?' I was aflush with sentiment and wanted to cover up. 'You want to watch I don't get straddled across you one night.'

That broke the spell (damn it!). Rufus was a bit indignant. 'Naw! Not like that Ke . . . we're family.'

Wed. 12th

Catch myself off guard sometimes using American idiom in a phoney accent.

Great hubbub about Mrs Grey's jewellery. Police have been called in and everyone's got to make a statement.

Have just finished the hedges though they wouldn't stand the test of a spirit level. Sister T (who *must* look like Heloise) wheeling an old dear round the grounds for her birthday. Cut her (the old dear) a rose as a present and gave her a peck. The others oohed and aahed like schoolgirls.

Placid and tranquil like a slow stream in a sunny valley . . . like those Inca women in Barranca suckling their young in the market square.

. . . Rufus on my mind . . .

Thurs. 13th

Interviewed by the police this morning. Told them all I know – nothing.

Took Rufus up to Agnes's flat. (Neither knew of the other's existence.) Father Michael was there. Good evening all round. Strange to see Agnes the social widow. I've been thinking of her more as a mattress.

She made a strong point of avoiding any familiarity toward me so as not to arouse Father Michael's suspicions. All her charm and beauty – and she has a surplus of both – were put on display for Rufus who thought she was chatting him up. It flatters him to be chatted up and once he has a fish on his line he'll play it to the death.

But you wouldn't know this from his off-hand manner . . .

(I can tell by the way he stresses his nationality . . . noticed it when Betty met him the other morning and kept repeating ' . . . An' you a real live 'Merikeen . . . ' It sets him apart, distinguishes him. He even laughs.)

Father Michael paid a lot of attention to Rufus too. He obviously thinks we're having it away with each other and watched for signs and portents. Didn't get any though. He watched Agnes, as well, to see if she noticed any electricity between Rufus and me.

Suspicious quartet! (Except for Rufus who was blandly unaware of the calculations going on around him. His chief concern was to throw me a disguised SOS with those grey eyes of his whenever he foundered in conversational shallows.)

Why can't human beings all be open with each other . . . ? (OK, let me learn . . .)

During the conversation Agnes asked me something and I said I didn't know. In his clipped humorous tone Father Michael said 'Keiron knows nothing that doesn't concern sex; Keiron's obsessed with sex . . . '

Was a bit choked at the time but thinking about it I guess he's right.

I *am* pretty hung-up on sex . . .

But hell, I was born into a pretty sex-obsessed society . . .

It's not so much the act as the *need* . . .

In all hell's chambers I reckon the one reserved for those who drowned their souls in lust will be the least populated. There's a sort of saturation point where man, the animal, comes crawling back to God and that's not so true of the proud man, the vain man, the power hungry, the hate-consumed . . .

The bulk of fornicators are, at least, looking for love . . .

Fri. 14th

Court this morning. We didn't wake up till half eight. Rufus drove me back here for the boiler then down to the Court House off East India Dock Road for half ten.

Pete waiting on steps in the sun. Twenty or thirty people hanging around and he was pretty chuffed when we pulled up in the Aston-Martin and went in with him. He was the first called. Rufus and me stood in a miserable little pew at the back and watched him come out and stand on this platform.

I knew he was nervous as hell but he put on a good front as if he went to court every day.

The cops who drink at his local had got in touch with the lot who pulled him and when the charge was read it sounded almost apologetic. Mentioned that he's getting married next week and all. The magistrate was a kindly-looking old Jew.

The fine and the doctor's fee only came to twenty-five quid but Pete loses his licence for a year. Luckily he was able to flog his egg shipment to another geezer though he lost on it. Told him to keep the money he borrowed as a wedding-present.

We went to a boozer after. Pete still doesn't like Rufus but he was prepared to tolerate him for the sake of the motor. When Rufus left the bar for a slash Pete said quickly 'You avoidin' me lately? Wot's the matter? If fis marriage lark's bovverin' you – forget it. It's not changin' me any . . .'

I didn't know what to say. I said 'Come off it Pete, don't be daft! I thought you'd be busy doing a Romeo and making plans and that . . . I'd look a right cunt pushing in there. Anyway I've been knocking around with the Yank just lately and you don't seem to take to him much.'

Pete mused. 'You havin' it away with that geezer or sumpin'?'

'No. Not like you're thinking.'

' 'E's wimperin' round you like a bleedin' 'ound.'

'Thought it was me doing the whimpering. I'm pretty chuffed with him really . . . '

'Well don't go bringin' 'im to the nupshals – the bird'll 'ave a miscarriage.'

Rang Penny but she can't get off work. Taking Agnes though I'll feel a bit ashamed. Can always pass her off as my mother.

Bit pissed. No temper for writing . . .

Fri. 15th

Full day yesterday. Fragments I noted at the time scatter about my mind like litter before a wind.

I get so pissed, that's the trouble.

Chronologically:

After yesterday's entry Yoop rings to say *Swallows* is published. (I'd almost forgotten about it.) I meet him at the club. He looks terrible, as if he's going through some private hell. His skin is white and sunken, hair and forehead damp with sweat. Eyes tortured. I ask what's wrong and he says with a trace of I-don't-know-what, 'Ask me again in ten years Keiron.' Drugs I expect.

We talk about the magazine and he says Horror Face has a copy for me. He wants to meet me.

The doorman leads me to a suite on the top floor of Gallaby's, knocks and scrams.

'Come in Keiron.' I go in.

He is lounging on the arm of a settee, dangling an elbow across the back. He wears a smoking-jacket affair and the back of his head and part of his face are artfully concealed behind a white scarf. The exposed skin is thick with make-up.

He stares at me for a long time. His eyes are clear and commanding. I determine not to be put out but you sure know he's looking at you.

He's holding a copy of *Ganymede*. He hands it to me and says 'Your story is out today. It looks well in print.' (His voice is slow and calm and invites confidence, nothing like I'd imagined.) I say 'Thanks' and sit down. It seems strange that this is the first exchange of words between us. A casual observer would imagine we'd been on speaking-terms for years.

The story does look well. It is finely, if erotically, illustrated and there's my picture in a little box with a spiel which makes me sound like Billy Budd.

He hands me a drink and eventually says 'Well, what do you think of it?' I say I'm chuffed, etc.

Then he says 'You must think me a dreadful old pervert . . .'

I say I do.

He starts pacing around the room.

I say I'm joking and a meandering monologue about how I remind him of someone follows. All a bit heavy.

I was pissed enough when I got there and the way he keeps topping my glass up doesn't help any. He talks on, getting more and more emotional . . .

His drift is that he could do all sorts of wonderful things for Rufus and me if I'd let him (he sure is well briefed on my private life) so I more or less say OK, go ahead and do wonderful things . . . I'm not stopping you . . .

I mean if he wants to live vicariously it might as well be through me as anyone else – especially as he includes Rufus. At one point Rufus and me (I) were established in a secluded villa on the Mediterranean from where I churned out pages of sparkling prose . . . very Maugham . . . the booze went down well too . . .

When the time is ripe he produces porny photos, mostly colourful single poses though towards the end some highly stylised tableaux of group sodomy emerge.

Affect to take little interest but I'm a lousy actor.

Before I know it of course he's down gobbling me which is all right if I concentrate on the pictures and not on him.

Left almost immediately after with a promise to ring today.

Felt sorry for the old cunt really; he's not as repulsive as I'd thought . . . not if you don't look at him anyway.

It niggles me in sobriety but surely there can't be any evil in letting a fella go down on you when he's so desperate for it. I reckon no one else'd be soft enough and it means nothing to me. Besides, I didn't take any money for it.

Downstairs I drink at the bar. Rufus is there with an epicene German. Can't resist showing off *Swallows* then curse myself because in a way it could rift us. But he doesn't know this. He's in high spirits and wants to celebrate. We'll go somewhere real smart and make like lords . . .

I say 'What about your mate?' pointing at the German and he's all a-pother.

'Aw, sheet man . . . say, I won't be a minute . . . no! Screw him!'

'You'd best see what he's worth . . . '

'Fuck eeet! One minute Ke . . . I won't be more'n one minute . . . ' and with thoughtless brutality he calls 'Come on Kraut' to the German as he strides towards the lift.

Drank everywhere after that and got so pissed we had to leave the motor and taxi back to Russel Square.

This morning I was still half shot. We were lying there talking (it was pretty pleasant) with arms and legs all tangled up and as I was trying to manoeuvre so's he wouldn't notice I'd a thumping great hard on he said, 'What'd you used to do when those guys tried to kiss you Ke?'

'Kissed them back.'

'No, I mean like when they wanna stick their tongue down your throat an' that.'

'If that's what they're paying for . . . '

'Yea but . . . '

I couldn't resist it. His chin was resting on my shoulder and his mouth, quivering with questions, was so near that I leaned down and kissed him. He didn't try to stop me or anything but he didn't co-operate either. I could sense he was none too pleased.

Disentangled myself and turned away from him. (To be honest I felt a bit of a cunt.)

He turned himself then and said, 'You're not sore at me are you Ke?'

I said, 'No, I got a hard on, that's all.'

He said, 'What for?'

I said, 'How the hell do I know what for? It just came.'

He moved forward and sort of hunched his elbows over my shoulders. 'Hey Ke, don't be sore at me. You can kiss me all you want. You can screw me if you wanna, you're the only guy I'd let, but sheet man, we're brothers, ain't we?'

Hell of a long silence.

'We wouldn't be brothers no more Ke . . . see what I mean?'

God! Wish I was a eunuch or something.

Sat. 16th

Article on Bergotte in the *Telegraph*. He's in London for the publication of a new book so I've posted off to him at his publishers saying I'd written before and it'd be a privilege to meet him, etc. I don't know, it somehow looks like you're after something when you write to a stranger because he's a celebrity . . .

Then again I can't really think of Bergotte as a stranger . . .

Cool day, nothing much to report. Life in the convent buzzes on like a well ordered hive.

In the rose-garden a tap drips irregularly into a drain as big as a well. At the bottom the water tinkles and echoes and the sound is silver, like music from a barrel-organ. The roses shuffle to it.

Horror Face wants Rufus and me to go and stay at Virginia Water for a few days. I'm easy but will have to see Rufus. Reckon he'll latch on to the project though – that Aegean (or was it Mediterranean?) villa is shaping into reality in his mind.

. . . Must stop calling Horror Face *Horror Face* or I'll find myself saying it in front of him one of these days . . .

Manicomio is taking on new life . . .

Wonder if Bergotte . . . or would that be asking too much . . . ?

Sun. 17th

Sundays no longer lustreless . . . Rufus gives them dimension . . .

Dawn this morning a new creation. Dim grim grimy London, sleeping like a bum on a park bench, was stirred suddenly, rinsed with water-colours and clothed in a rainbow of oils. Ships, towers, domes, temples and theatres . . . the richness and variety. Serene peace on the streets and between warehouses. Innocence most pronounced on waking.

We couldn't sleep and drove round in it. On the weed half the night, then talking. Dozed then rose and drove off into the dawn. Parked near Temple and watched the river change colour.

Didn't speak. Breathless and eternal. Sometimes I feel more affection for that fella than this frame seems capable of housing. Wish we were both dead and in heaven with God; that everything was pure and permanent.

Back here morning has crowded through the windows and the essence of it lodges like a soul in the glass of the mermaid, radiant and serene.

Have given it to Rufus.

Midday. Off now to Virginia Water. Hope I can remember the entrance.

Half wish I wasn't going. It's plain old prostitution whatever you call it. Rufus rabid for profits . . .

Dawdling now, waiting for motor. Is it my imagination or are the roses withering in the rose-garden . . . ?

Hated asking Reverend Mother if it'd be OK for me to shoot off for another day or two. It's too much for a woman shovelling all that coal. Still, she doesn't mind. She laughs and says 'Oh, Keiron, I wish I was young again . . .'

If only she knew it she's younger than I ever was . . .

Therapeutic writing . . .

It is past midnight and the convent is asleep. The air is warm. Moths flap hideously around the electric light. I have drawn the curtains so that strangers on the High Street cannot see the turmoil in my room. Besides, I don't want to see them. I don't want to see anyone.

My mind is a riot of voices, arguing, shouting, screaming . . .
I am temporarily rattled but *I am not going mad.*
I must be patient. Must wait, be calm, be rational . . .
My interference will only aggravate the fury of the voices . . .
Eventually they will kill each other and I will be at peace . . .
If I listen to them they will kill me . . .

Next week, next year, all this will be pale memory.

Am smoking a cigarette, the last of Rufus's kit. It will cool the
nerves, help me consider what to do with this casket.

There is a way out of everything if one is cool . . .

. . . Necklaces of gold filagree, incredibly intricate, mythical
spider's-webs dripping pearls instead of dew . . . rings with stones
as huge as eggs; pure, opaque, speckled, set in elephant saddles and
plaited platinum . . . coins and chains and dragons with emerald
eyes and scales of ivory . . .

A tiara so splendid, so simple it challenges words (yet it floats
before my eyes when I close them) . . .

The casket a gem-studded camphor-wood box (so old it smells
of the sea) . . .

Pellets of diamonds like the Virgin's tears . . .

A rosary of rubies with a greenstone cross . . .

An ebony Christ . . .

(Could they buy innocence back . . . ?)

The monster I've become . . .

WOMAN PLUNGES TO DEATH
ON FARLEY ROAD

Mrs Agnes Coulson (née Macfarlane) of Quintock was killed instantly last night when her Volkswagen plunged into the ravine on the disused stretch of the Farley Road just south of the Killiepool Pass.

Mrs Coulson who has been living in London for the past decade will be best remembered in the community as a co-founder of the Quintock Amateur Choral and Operatic Group and for many years their lead soprano.

Mrs Coulson was a widow, her husband, Mr Edward Coulson of Bootle, Lancs, having tragically met his death with the sinking of the naval auxiliary vessel *Tidepond* in the Far East only four months ago. A report of the event and an obituary were printed in this paper at the time.

Mrs Coulson is survived by two children, Mark 6, and Richard 2. Her mother Mrs Helen Macfarlane lives at 26 Redfern Drive, Quintock.

The funeral service will be conducted at St Andrew's Parish Church on Friday next at 10 a.m.

Dear Father Michael,

How do you start a letter you've put off writing for so many months?

Just start I guess.

Your letter, with cutting, and the Journal tracked me down in Hobart a few weeks ago after bouncing across continents. I was pretty surprised, I can tell you. Thought I'd burnt the Journal along with *Manicomio* and my other papers that feverish night I went back to the convent and here it turns up like the ghost of my past sins. What I can't figure is how you found what ship I was on. Thought my tracks had been well covered. Can only suppose you heard from Agnes's mother too.

Yes, I did know, Father. Her mother wrote me a pretty touching letter saying how highly Agnes had spoken of me as a friend of Eddie's and if anything should ever happen to her, etc. It was just like her to arrange her own death to cause no inconvenience to anybody else . . .

(Hell, I don't want to talk about her. I'd have so much to say I'd never stop. I feel like a murderer. Believe me, I've been through months of it . . .)

You shouldn't apologise for reading the Journal, Father. I asked you to once if you remember and you refused but the offer still held. At least it supplies the background to my pretty shameful exit from the convent.

You suggest I might offer explanations for my movements, etc. Guess you have a right to demand some really . . .

The days we spent at Horror Face's were OK, nothing to rave about, just drinking, swimming, watching movies and lounging around. We were left pretty much to ourselves come to think of it but we never knew when the old boy wasn't staring from some window or haunting the trees near the pool. It was eerie sometimes, especially when you looked up suddenly and saw that face. Rufus said it reminded him of those public lavatories where perverts peer through holes.

Found out a bit about him there – Horror Face I mean. He really *was* rich, tycoon class – not one of Guernsey's either! Winchell's and Gallaby's and *Ganymede* were only a hobby. His disfigurement was a wartime burn, he told me that himself. Said his whole body was a charred mass. Apparently he was burnt out of a house resistance-fighting in Holland. Yoop's mother and father (he's the one I'm supposed to remind Horror Face of) died in the same blaze. After the war he adopted Yoop. Something like that.

He was kind to us, in fact he couldn't have done more for visiting royalty but always I felt like the pampered Pekingese being required to return dog affection to its master. That's not me. I can't be subservient. I can hire myself around but can't sell outright. Not even for Horror Face's money.

He cottoned on to this after a couple of days too and I think it dimmed his ardour a bit. He began to take more of an interest in Rufus, and Rufus was so inscrutable when he wanted to be that Horror Face never knew where he stood with him.

On the Thursday evening Rufus and I (me sounds better) got drunk. We'd downed a whole bottle of vodka between us and were well into the second when Rufus started talking about Pete. He was saying that Pete didn't like him and he couldn't understand why. He was thinking of buying him a wedding present, something smart, to show there was no ill will on his part . . .

Pete! The wedding! It been and gone. I'd forgotten: hadn't given it a thought; *and I was to have been best man* . . .

Oh hell Father, I can tell you I felt bloody lousy; worse than lousy, I just wanted to disintegrate. I'd never felt so miserable, low, contemptible in all my life before. It wasn't even treachery à la Genet. I was just selfish . . . selfish, ignorant and weak . . .

I'd go on for pages if I tried to put down the thoughts that crowded my mind at the time but they did produce a clear resolve. I left the house. Just as I was walked to the main road and hitched a lift to Heathrow. From there I took a bus to Kensington.

It was late when I arrived at the convent and I didn't see

anyone. My mind was in chaos, a sort of drunken claustrophobia
. . . I was sepulchred in the universe and had to keep moving to
find a way out.

I stumbled about throwing things into my grip. There was
ten times more gear than there was packing space. I was fuming
with impatience and swearing. I tumbled the contents of the
drawers and wardrobe over the bed and started to rummage.
Next I know I've got the lid off a strange box and am face to
face with the jewels. Fantastic they were. I jotted down some of
the pieces that struck me then so you probably know what I
mean. You never see stuff like that in shop-windows.

I stood and stared at them for a long while. What was I to do
with them? I was scared. I even convinced myself I'd stolen
them. I was jolted, then desperate, then potty.

Remember scribbling those last lines in the Journal then
taking all my papers across to the boiler and feeding them to the
flames with a destructive fixity that would have shamed Hedda
Gabler.

When all my gear was bundled together I threw it into a taxi
and retreated to Agnes's place. I took the casket with me and
saw the police in every shadow on the way. Poor Agnes! I told
her God knows what lies and threatened her against telling you
that I was at the flat.

The following day I got this ship off the Pool – a fly-out job
for Genoa on the Tuesday.

What a weekend! I spent money like Death had sent me a
cable and was paralytic most of the time. If I thought at all it
was about Rufus, nauseating self-pitying thoughts which
needed to be drowned in gallons of booze. Worst was taking
Tom back to Agnes's on the Saturday afternoon. She had to go
out and I'd promised to look after the kids. When she came
home she found us turned in together. She never said a word.
Tom even stayed the night. Next morning she brought us
breakfast and shuffled the kids into the motor and drove off to
her mother's in Scotland.

As I kissed her goodbye she whispered, or rather whimpered,
'Do I turn men away from women? Keiron, tell me . . . what's
wrong with me? Keiron, where do I go wrong? Eddie, you . . .

will the children grow up to hate me ... ?' She was shaking and I should have seen that she'd reached the rock-bottom of despair. I had to push her away before she broke down. I said 'Don't be daft darling, we all love you'.

She said 'But ... ' and Richard started crying.

That was the last time I saw her.

(Yes. I'll force myself to tell you. Complete the picture sort of. I let Tom fuck me that Saturday night which doesn't matter too much I suppose, put it down to experience, but – and here I'm sweating over writing this – we're a week at sea and I find I've got a dose up the arse. Tried to convince myself it was a thousand other things till Cape Town where they rammed a tube up me and confirmed the worst. It's OK now of course, just a few injections and the bug went. Suppose it was justice in a way ... can't expect to play with fire, etc ...)

On the Sunday night I met Bergotte. He'd answered my note so I rang and arranged to meet him. Tried to sober up but it was useless. Agnes had ironed a shirt and left it ready. Cut myself in three places shaving and didn't know my collar was patched with blood till I met him in a bar in Sloane Square.

Made a fool of myself from the start. Was harassed about the blood and was trying too hard not to appear drunk. Confoundedly star-struck as well. He must have thought I was some sort of nut.

He took me to dinner in a place along the King's Road and answered all my questions so patiently that I mistook his fortitude for interest and plunged on.

He was smaller than I'd imagined and fine-looking too – almost boyish really. What I admired most was his casual modesty. I can understand a set and studied deference after a lifetime of fame (guess it would be indispensable) but his wasn't like that. It rang true every time. I had the feeling that fame had taught him simplicity, that it had taught him how art is distinct from the artist, how the artist mustn't appropriate the praise which is offered to his art ... but you haven't read my Bergotte have you, so I'm rambling!

The night before flying out I took the casket to Russell Square. I let myself into the flat. Rufus wasn't there. He obviously hadn't come back from Virginia Water.

I left the jewels on his table with a note explaining how Mrs Grey must have meant me to have them but that there was no way of proving it. They weren't hot, I said, because no one knew what they looked like or even that they existed. Suggested they might help towards his millions.

Mentioned that I was shipping out and wished him luck.

. . . And all the while, behind the thin screen of reality, cameras were trained on me. They were shooting the climax to an updated *Camille*. Clash of cymbals. Doleful, vibrating notes from the violins. Gosh, how much simpler life would be if we weren't conditioned by the movies . . .

Well that's about it, Father. That was Sodom.

Have just re-read your letter. Your comments on the Journal are pretty good, pretty revealing really. Humbling too, though you seem more concerned with my syntax than with my morals. It was only an exercise Father, a discipline, and invariably rushed. Too much said . . . so many weeds . . .

I'm keeping another Journal on this ship but I've developed a few theories and set myself lines to work on. Am trying to avoid the obvious, meaningful touches like Gide not mentioning the 1918 armistice or the fragmentary Waterloo in *Charterhouse of Parma* . . . the Gospels . . .

I reckon a Journal should be unselfconscious even if it *is* about self. It should be a writer's studio, workshop, rehearsal-room; a gymnasium where he keeps in training and has his falls. It should be free like a wild boar roaming where it fancies, burrowing its snout into the most unlikely roots on its path.

Yes, I suppose I do write in two idioms; but then I live on two planes. I can't even begin to develop a strict style. Don't want to either. I want to paint reds with red and blues with blue and be able (when I've learned how) to mix new shades from old colours. Is that obscure? . . . Guess I just keep mixing!

You're right about the poetry though; I'll never be able to kid myself I'm a poet.

Can't suppress a smile when I read your reference to my *Irish heritage*. What lies did I tell you? Or were you mislead by the name? Before me it belonged to the last kid to die in the

Stepney Home where I was an unclaimed bundle. Or so I've always been told.

Pretty anonymous huh!

It's almost midnight and there's my call for the watch – four hours of savage amusement as Pete used to say. (Pete! How the hell am I going to face him when the time comes? Haven't even had the guts to write yet.) Alternate hours solitary on the wing of the bridge contemplating infinity to satisfy some bizarre libido of the Board of Trade.

What a devilish, frolicsome way to ring the New Year in.

Will finish this letter off when I come down, Father . . .

It's a pleasure more than a task on the bridge right now. The last albatross has turned back and the winds are growing warm. The moon hangs gleaming like a chandelier and the stars sparkle with a brilliance down here they never show over Europe.

It's nights like this I live for. You know, fellas like me shouldn't be allowed ashore for any length of time. We're like those monkeys I read about in *Life* – peaceful ordered animals in their native state which grow vicious and destroy themselves when zooed . . . hold on, I'm going to fetch myself a mug of tea . . .

Already the New Year is hatching along the brink of the ocean. The fellas are still singing *Auld Lang Syne* in the cook's cabin but the voices are gathering moss. There'll be a few bad heads later in the day.

It's a bit of a drag watch-keeping; not being able to join the festivities I mean, but I'll do my celebrating in Yokohama when we get there.

Don't do much drinking on the ship anyhow. It's pretty quiet at sea. Most of the fellas are married with kids and saving up to live happily ever after. My social activities are confined to playing *Scrabble* in the mess-room after tea. It's not much fun though 'cause I always win.

But don't think I'm complaining; I love the life. Outside

working hours I hermit myself in the cabin here with my books and kind of drift along contentedly.

I commit my sins in port.

. . . Another mug of char . . .

Had planned some electric pages on the bridge just now but, as always when confronted with the blank sheet, the current switches off . . .

Wanted to tell you how radically my attitude to a lot of things (God, sex, love, myself) has changed and is changing since we last spoke.

Wanted to ask if you'd seen Rufus and if so how he was and if he'd asked for me. The worst of it's passed, like Anna-Greta's cold, but it's still there, deep down, dormant, waiting to surface on the lonely nights . . . and then the ache starts. You know sometimes I catch a glimpse of a fella with Rufus's swagger walking in the street, or in a bar, say, with hair combed the same as his and everything in me melts liquid and I all but cry out. Don't reckon I could ever feel that way about anyone again . . .

Funny how we can't even begin to explain these things. There are so many secrets (like the knowledge of good and evil and the certainty of God) that all the millions and millions of us carry in endless procession from birth to death but can't communicate. Strange that! You'd think it wouldn't be a secret any more when everybody knew about it.

Wanted to tell you about Yvonne in Vancouver, the only girl I ever met I reckon I'd like to marry. She's no great beauty and she doesn't know a thing about books but she's my idea of a woman . . . sort of like Fanny Price in *Mansfield Park* if you know what I mean. I didn't think they turned them out like that any more . . .

But it'd be useless! I'd be kidding her, I'd be kidding myself.

I'm upwards from halfway bent . . . I pretty well got to accept it now. It doesn't trouble me too much. I only ever wanted to be myself and if that's me, well then – that's me! I'd rather find out now than when I'm middle-aged with half-a-dozen kids and be forced to live a furtive life around public toilets or paying for it in Gallaby's.

No! This martyred acceptance of the Fates is a platitude. If

I'm going to be honest I might as well start by suspecting *me*. You know Father, beyond the ramparts I've built to exonerate myself I hear an accusing whisper which tells me I've brought it all on my own head. A fella can't be blamed if he's born like that, I mean if he's a queen, or if something in his mind or body has made him go like that but I rushed into the trap for giggles, for kicks, for the attentions which fanned my ego and now I'm ensnared.

A bird's still best for sex (it never was much cop with a fella) but somehow they don't interest me too much any more. There's a wall between us. I've lost the hunter instinct.

I don't know, maybe it's just a phase . . . but even after I'd been with Yvonne I'd get her to drop me off in Grenville Street then do all the queer bars along there and shack up with the first smooth-skinned kid who told me I was strong and handsome.

Had a bird in Brisbane too and used to do much the same with her. Since then I've more or less dropped the birds.

Still looking for Dansk I guess – even if in the wrong direction.

Funny thing is – I don't want to change . . .

That day-trip I took to Sodom came to be a regular journey. Not just Sundays but Mondays, Tuesdays, Wednesdays . . . I don't even commute any more . . .

I'm a citizen.

I have bought Beauty in the markets
And snared it in the wilds of the world;
Lips cheating destiny with a kiss too eager,
Youth wide-eyed with the inexpressible . . .

I have searched faces where the heart was sparked
And frisked the limbs of lust for answers . . .

But all have kept strange silence as if to tell me:
Feed on loneliness as the cow feeds from its own belly.

Wrote that in a spasm of alcoholic remorse after a wild spree in Manila. But it doesn't tell a full truth because I know part of the answer myself. The very futility of the homosexual life fosters, in me at any rate, an awareness of God and a faith in Christianity. I bought a book called the *Dutch Catechism* to try to come to grips with Catholicism and find it mighty. Sometimes it affects me so much that I want to grab a priest and say 'Baptize me quick, I'm going to be the best Catholic that ever was'. Then I go to bed and put my arms around the pillow and call it Rufus.

What I want to know is how a fella's supposed to reconcile the two. Seems you've got to be either sexless or a saint to be a Catholic.

Or am I naïve or something? Or weaker or freakier than everybody else. Or am I beginning to understand what you meant by *torment* now?

(But, fuck it Father – it's not always lust . . .)

Here, I'm getting heavy, mixed-up, boorish. I'm tired. I've got to turn-to again at nine.

I wanted to ask you about the nuns, and Betty and the old dears . . . wanted to know if I'm under a cloud with Reverend Mother or if she's forgiven me without knowing what she's forgiving . . . wanted to ask so many things but the pen's dropping out of my hand.

Will write again from Japan.

> Friendship endures,
> Keiron Dorrity.

P.S. When you're in contact with Upstairs put in a word for the Hero; his armour's rusting . . . and for Agnes; though I reckon she's made it, don't you?

On the following pages are other recent paperbacks
published by Quartet Books.
If you would like a complete catalogue of
Quartet's publications please
write to us at 27 Goodge Street, London W1P 1FD

WALK DON'T WALK
Gordon Williams

By the bestselling author of *The Straw Dogs*, *The Man Who Had Power Over Women* and *The Camp*.

'Hugely successful . . . this is a swiftly paced, finely written novel, and it's a great deal of fun' – *The Times*

'Extremely funny . . . It is a pleasure to recommend a book that flies higher than its blurb' – *New Statesman*

Fiction 40p

HOLDING ON
Mervyn Jones

By the author of *John and Mary* and *Mr Armitage Isn't Back Yet*.

The bestselling saga of an ordinary family's struggle for survival in a world of war, poverty and turbulent change.

'A warm-hearted, sinewy, immensely readable book – it is also, unobtrusively, an honest and admirable portrait of working-class life and ideals' – *Birmingham Post*

Holding On has been serialised on radio and is to be a television series on London Weekend Television in 1975.

Fiction 60p

THE FORT
John Hale

A novel of outstanding power about freedom – political, sexual, marital, personal – and what can happen in the pursuit of it by the award-winning playwright, scriptwriter, producer and novelist.

'Carries one excitedly along . . . it's the action that counts' – *Bristol Evening Post*

'The narrative, especially the scenes of action is well done . . . an honest and well-executed book' – *Financial Times*

Fiction 50p

ANY NUMBER CAN PLAY
Dennis Bloodworth

'A lusciously written novel . . . crammed tight with revelations, cross-purposes, disguises and black comedy . . . and for good measure there is the most hilarious sex marathon one could hope to read' – *Scotsman*

'A South-East Asian thriller, worth speaking of in the same breath as *The Quiet American*' – *Times Literary Supplement*

'As macabre and as exciting, as sad and as complex and as alluring as Indo-China itself . . . infinitely more enjoyable than most novels' – *Sunday Times*

Fiction 40p

THE PROTO PAPERS
Philip Oakes

Only three of them really know what is going on. Two are mad. The third is a huge, vicious chimpanzee

'Much more than immensely readable and exciting; it is intelligent and precision built . . . we shall be lucky to get any novel this year or next as absorbing and as open-eyed as this one' – *The Times*

'As a piece of speculative fiction, imaginative though rooted in scientific fact, this is a very readable adventure, sharply written, with many poetic touches, and of course sexy touches too. Very intelligent and racey' – *Sunday Times*

Fiction 50p

THE ORGANIZATION
Philip Mackie

Richard Pershore considers himself bright, dynamic and promising; just the kind of young man a giant industrial complex like Greatrick needs. But once on the inside as a junior executive, he soon realizes what 'qualities' are really required by the Organization.

'Cynical fantasy, demonstrating just how appalling the rat-race is to compete in, but how enjoyable it is to observe from the outside. The jokes are knowing but credible, the characters familiar but intriguing, and the whole organization ticks over like a presentation gold watch' – Alan Brien, *Sunday Times*

Based on Philip Mackie's own award-winning television series.

Fiction 50p

SUMMER COMING
Jane Gaskell

‚Jane Gaskell shines like a naughty deed in a good grey world’ –
Guardian

‘Jane Gaskell is always sharp, funny and bitchy; her characters
can’t afford to be thin-skinned and neither can her readers’ –
Cosmopolitan

‘It is well established that Jane Gaskell ... is a story-teller
of driving power, uncomfortable invention and reckless
psychological subtlety’ – *Daily Telegraph*

Fiction 40p

This book is obtainable from booksellers and newsagents
or can be ordered direct from the publishers. Send a cheque
or postal order for the purchase price plus 6p postage and
packing to Quartet Books Limited, P.O. Box 11, Falmouth,
Cornwall TR10 9EN